unbreak
my
heart

ALSO BY MELISSA WALKER

Small Town Sinners

unbreak my heart

MELISSA WALKER

BLOOMSBURY

NEW YORK BERLIN LONDON SYDNEY

First published in the United States of America in
May 2012 by Bloomsbury Books for Young Readers
www.bloomsburyteens.com

For information about permission to
reproduce selections from this book, write to
Permissions, Bloomsbury BFYR, 175 Fifth Avenue,
New York, New York 10010

Library of Congress Cataloging-in-Publication Data
Walker, Melissa (Melissa Carol).
Unbreak my heart / by Melissa Walker. — 1st U.S. ed.
            p.   cm.
Summary: Taking the family sailboat on a summer-long trip
excites everyone except sixteen-year-old Clementine,
who feels stranded with her parents and younger sister
and guilty over a falling-out with her best friend.
ISBN 978-1-59990-528-0 (hardcover)
[1. Boats and boating—Fiction. 2. Family life—Fiction.
3. Best friends—Fiction. 4. Friendship—Fiction.] I. Title.
PZ7.W153625Un 2011   [Fic]—dc23   2011032347

Book design by Regina Roff
Typeset by Westchester Book Composition
Printed in the U.S.A. by Quad/Graphics, Fairfield, Pennsylvania
1 2 3 4 5 6 7 8 9 10

All papers used by Bloomsbury Publishing, Inc., are natural, recyclable products
made from wood grown in well-managed forests. The manufacturing processes
conform to the environmental regulations of the country of origin.

For June,
who has my heart

unbreak
my
heart

chapter one

"Sit on it," I say.

"Excuse me?" asks Olive, with an attitude that makes her seem way older than her ten years. Her tone plus her big angular glasses—green-framed rectangles that look more fancy-architect than fifth-grade—put her somewhere near forty in my book. She's always been our family's little adult.

"The suitcase, Livy," I say sweetly. "Please?"

My sister reluctantly plops down on top of my raggedy plaid bag. It moves just enough so that I can zip it shut.

"Thanks."

"You better get it downstairs right now," says Olive, running ahead of me into the hallway. "The car's almost full."

I sigh and take one more glance around my room. It looks just like it always does—sunny, bright, clean; a bookshelf along the back wall filled with rows and rows of the series I love; a white wicker hamper in the corner with a stray gray sweatshirt on top of it; the flower-covered comforter I've publicly outgrown but that secretly makes me feel safe. I grab my journal off the nightstand

and shove it into the front pocket of my bag. If I'm not going to have Internet or phone service for most of the summer, I need *somewhere* to record my status updates.

I stare in the big mirror across from my bed. My hair hangs down around my face, and my eyes are still a little puffy from crying. I pinch my cheeks to make them pink and try a smile. It looks more like the grimace of someone trying to pretend she's not in pain. I frown again. At least frowns are honest.

I heave the suitcase off my bed. I'm going away for three months, but this is the only bag I'm allowed to bring, because I'll be living on a boat. With my family. All. Summer. Long.

If my sophomore year had gone differently, I probably would have fought harder to spend this summer—the summer I turned sixteen, the summer of making out, the summer of memories that will last forever, the summer I always imagined would be the *very best one*—at home on my own. I'm responsible, after all, and my parents trust me. I could have had an amazing time working days at Razzy's, the Bishop Heights Mall candy shop where I had a job this year, looking for my it's-just-like-in-the-movies perfect guy, and spending nights hanging out with Amanda . . . *Amanda*.

I feel a stone drop in my stomach.

I head downstairs, letting my big bag *plunk, plunk, plunk* on each step.

"There she is," says Mom, smiling brightly. "Little Miss Sunshine."

I don't smile back. She's being sarcastic, and she's wearing a giant floppy straw hat, the kind that only almost-famous girls in LA and very old ladies in Florida can pull off. I guess now that she's less lawyer and more boater she thinks it works. She is wrong.

Dad comes around to the back of the car and slides my bag into the one slot that's left. It fits perfectly, and he sighs with satisfaction. It's a real thrill for him when the sport wagon is well packed.

"How good is your dad?" he asks me.

"You have sunscreen on your nose," I say to him.

He smiles and rubs it in. Nothing is penetrating the parents' Good Mood today, not even me being grumpy. I guess they're getting used to it.

I wasn't always such a downer. Up until, like, two weeks ago, I was Clementine Williams, happy and upbeat and kind of hilarious, if I do say so myself. But that was before everything exploded in my face.

Now I'm Clementine Williams, outcast. And that's on a good day.

"Come on, Clem," says Mom, putting her arm around me and easing me toward the car. She's been gentle with me this week, mostly, and I appreciate that.

I slide into the backseat next to Olive, who's squished against a cooler that's taking up most of our space. Good thing the drive to the marina is only twenty minutes.

"Let the Williams Family Summer of Boating begin!" cheers Dad. Mom gives a quick "Woot-woot," and Olive raises her hands in the air and shouts, "Wahoo!" I add an uninspired "Yay" so they won't get on my case. Then I stare out the window and watch my house, then my neighborhood, then my town, disappear.

⛵

As we pull into the marina, I see our boat—*The Possibility*. It's a forty-two-foot Catalina three-cabin Pullman. My parents traded in our twenty-three-foot O'Day—*Night Wind II*—last year, and they've been readying *The Possibility* for this summer trip since then. At first it felt insanely roomy compared to the *Night Wind II*,

3

where Olive and I basically had to sleep on narrow side couches in the main cabin of the boat. My parents' V-berth bedroom didn't even have a door, so my dad's snoring chased me out to the cockpit to sleep under the stars pretty often.

Yeah, the *Night Wind II* seemed small and *The Possibility* plenty big on quick weekend sails. I even brought Amanda up here a few times when Mom didn't come, and Dad let us have the master cabin so we could "stay up late and giggle," as he reductively put it. It was fun.

But now that I'm faced with the prospect of spending three whole months on this thing, it doesn't look very spacious. There are two *heads*—that means bathrooms—and three *staterooms*, which is a fancy word for teeny-tiny bedrooms. My parents have a master berth with their own head, and I have a double berth on the starboard side. Olive's port-side room has bunk beds, but she's still young enough to think that'll be fun. (Wait until she falls out when Dad anchors us too close to a main waterway, and the waves from passing ships knock her right on her butt. It's happened before.)

I lug the plaid bag into my *stateroom* and close the door. I just want to stretch out with my music for a while, so I put in earbuds and hope I won't be able to hear Mom when she starts bugging me to help unpack.

I hit Shuffle just to see what comes up, and when I hear the strains of "Beautiful Girl" by INXS, I feel a tear well in my eye. Like, instantly. I thought they'd all dried up, but no. I swear I deleted this playlist, but I must have had another copy of "Beautiful Girl" stored. I let myself be sad for thirty seconds, and then I angrily wipe away the tear.

My mom gives me exactly six minutes to be antisocial and unhelpful. I know because I get to listen to "Must I Paint You a

Picture?" by Billy Bragg, which is five and a half minutes long, and as it ends, I open my eyes to see Mom's messenger.

"You can't just bust into my room," I say to Olive, who has her hands on her hips and a stern look on her face, which is way too close to mine.

"Yes, I can," she says, pushing her angled glasses up on her nose. "These doors don't lock."

Her serious mouth breaks into a grin, like she knows she's going to get so much time with me this summer because we're in this majorly contained space and she can't help but show her total elation about that fact.

I soften a little.

"Mom needs you," she says.

"Fine." I stand up and make her scramble to get out of my way.

I march into the main cabin—well, I take three steps into the main cabin, anyway, passing my dad in the nav station port side—and there is my mother, organizing the canned foods in the *galley*, which normal people call the kitchen.

"Did you get pickles?" asks Olive, kneeling on the couch in front of the galley and leaning onto the bright yellow counter.

"Yes, I did, Little Miss Dill," says Mom.

"Yippee!" sings Olive. You'd think she won $100 on a scratch-off lotto card. Pickles get this reaction? My little sister is seriously high today.

"And I got the big marshmallows for you, Clem," says Mom, putting up the bag of Jet-Puffeds that I always request for adding to morning hot chocolate.

I nod. I do not *Yippee*.

I watch Mom put about fifty cans up into the top cabinet above the stove. She has a cookbook called *A Man, A Can, and a Plan*. Obviously, this book is for a twenty-two-year-old guy who hasn't learned to make a meal with real food yet, but Mom likes to call it "the Boat Cookbook." Creating a dinner entirely out of canned goods makes her feel really accomplished. "Besides," she told us when we had the "boat grocery list" family meeting last week, "canned goods keep for so long! We'll eat well every night."

I had nodded then—I'd just wanted to be released from the family meeting so I could go back to my room and mope—but now, as I watch the cans of peas, pinto beans, and SpaghettiOs come out of her box, I wonder if I should have stood up for some fresher foods.

"What do you need me to help with?" I ask. I try to keep any sort of "tone" out of my voice. It's not my family's fault I've become a pariah.

"You could make sure everything's out of the car and then drive it over to long-term parking," says Mom. "It'll be your last chance to break in that license for a while."

"Okay," I say. And then, to Olive, "Come on."

My sister smiles widely and I stare back at her and try to look remotely friendly. I owe it to her to let her tag along, especially since I've been nasty all week.

Mom hands me the car keys, and Olive and I climb up the short ladder into the cockpit before carefully stepping off the boat and onto the dock.

I walk briskly toward the parking lot, and she jogs to keep up.

"Do you think Dad will let me unfurl the jib when we get underway?" she asks.

"Probably." My voice has a who-cares tone that I don't try to hide.

When we get to the car, Olive makes a big show of putting on her seat belt, even though we're only driving about a hundred feet to the long-term parking lot.

I give her a look and she says, "What? You've only been driving for, like, two weeks."

Two weeks exactly, actually. I got my license two Saturdays ago. That afternoon, I wanted to see who was around to go for a drive. I ended up texting Amanda and a few other people, but only one person responded right away. Unfortunately.

I pull into a spot in the shade and wrench up the parking brake.

"Nice," says Olive. "I didn't feel unsafe for a moment."

"I'm so glad." I step out of the car. When the sun hits my face, I close my eyes for a second to shake off the memory that's encroaching.

"Clem?"

I open my eyes and look down at my little sister, who's suddenly solemn.

"What?"

"I'm glad you've stopped crying."

I half smile at her. "Me too." I don't tell her that just because the tears have mostly dried up, it doesn't mean I'm better.

As we walk back to *The Possibility*, I see Mom unsnapping the blue canvas mainsail cover. Dad must want to get underway.

Before we go, though, I know we have to do one more thing.

I step back onto the boat and Dad pokes his head out from down below. "Ready?" he asks.

"Do we have a choice?" I ask.

"No!" Dad laughs really loudly. He is *so* happy right now. It's almost contagious. Almost.

Mom folds up the sail cover and sits down on the cockpit seat. Dad settles into his captain's chair, and Olive takes her perch next to him, the ultimate navigator. I sit back on the seat opposite Mom and tuck my legs underneath me.

"Now," starts Dad. "What do you see?"

He smiles and looks around at us. "Livy?"

My sister is still at an age where she's into this family game. Whenever we "embark on a new voyage"—which is my dad's fancy way of saying "go sailing" (you'd think we were heading into outer space)—we have to go around the cockpit and state what we want from the trip, what we see in our future days of sailing.

"I am ready for a really fun summer," says Olive. "I see swimming and fishing and cooking and eating and exploring islands."

Olive likes to jump off the boat when we anchor and swim to the closest land, which is usually some random mud-beach where there's nothing to do and no sand to lie out on. But I get it—I used to like that "explorer" game too.

"Excellent! All of that is very doable," says Dad. "Clem?"

"Mom can go."

"Okay," says Dad. "Julia?"

"I see a warm, wonderful summer filled with family days," says Mom. She's taken off her straw hat and is leaning her head back so her face catches the sun. Her brown hair is styled into that short Mom cut, but she also has these freckles that sometimes make her look really young when she smiles. Like now.

"Family time!" says Dad, clapping his hands together. "I love it! Clem?"

I look at my dad, who's smiling naively in my direction. He's treating us like we're his first-grade class. Suddenly I'm just annoyed. I'm sixteen years old. I don't need to sit here, being forced to do some roundtable "What I See" exercise with my way-younger sister and my dopey parents. This is their dream summer—not mine.

"Clem?" he asks again. "What do you see?"

"I see a summer in exile."

chapter two

We met on the first day of kindergarten, at the Play-Doh station. I was rolling a big blue ball in my hands, and Amanda asked to see it. Then she added a turned-up mouth and two eyes with her pieces of yellow clay.

After that, whenever anything made me sad, Amanda would say, "Do you need me to make you a smile?" She was like my friend–soul mate.

We talked about *everything*—from our first crushes in third grade to our late-arriving periods (Amanda got hers in eighth grade, I got mine in ninth)—while we sat on my bed and faced this big mirror on the opposite wall. We called it mirror-talking. My parents thought we were crazy, but there was something comforting about looking into the mirror at each other, and ourselves, while we talked. It made saying things easier somehow, just looking at reflections instead of the real person.

Maybe that's why, for the past week, I've been trying to write her a letter about what happened. I can't call her, and now that I'm stuck on this boat I certainly can't go see her. So I brought a whole pad of light green paper with my initials, CSW, in dark blue script at the top.

> Dear Amanda,
> How can you just forget the entire history of our friendship? Doesn't being best friends for over half our lives mean anything?

I crumple up the paper before I can write any more.

⛵

"Kidnap Picnic!" Amanda had yelled as I opened the door after she'd rung the bell three boisterous times in a row.

Last summer she had a tendency to show up unexpectedly with a plan for the day. Usually, I went with it.

She stood on our front porch in cutoffs, a striped T-shirt, and oversized sunglasses, and she carried a beach bag that was almost twice the size of her entire body.

"My mom dropped me off. I've got sandwiches, chips, two sodas, and four magazines," she said, walking past me through the door into the house. "But I forgot sunblock, so grab some when you go upstairs to get changed—forty-five or higher, please." She patted a rosy cheek. "I'm fair."

Amanda smiled and raised her sunglasses to the top of her head as she plopped down on the couch in the living room.

"I have to ask my—"

"Mr. and Mrs. Williams, Clem and I are going to the park!" she shouted, cupping her hands together like a megaphone. Then she grinned at me. "Done."

Ten minutes later, with a nod from my mom and just one round of "Why can't I go too?" whining from Olive—which was shut down by Dad telling her he'd take her to the pool instead—Amanda and I were heading for the park at the center of my neighborhood. We each took a handle of her giant bag of picnic supplies and walked straight to our usual spot—a central patch of grass in the sun where lots of people pass by as they cross from the soccer field to the ice cream truck.

"This way we can watch everyone, but people can also see *us*," she told me the first time we'd staked out this area two years earlier. Because this park was in walking distance of my house, our parents had been letting us "picnic" there since the summer we were thirteen.

I had traded my pajamas for a pair of bright red shorts and a white tank top, but as soon as we spread out the orange-and-blue-patterned blanket Amanda had brought for us to sit on, she peeled off her striped shirt to reveal a white triangle bikini top with multicolored butterflies on it.

My eyes must have gotten big, because she said, "This is why I really needed that sunblock."

It wasn't that people in the park didn't sometimes wear bikini tops, it was just that *we* never had. And my stiff beige bra under a boring plain white tank suddenly seemed really homely in comparison to what my best friend was wearing.

Amanda read all of these thoughts on my face. We were connected that way.

"Ooh, I should have told you I had on a bikini top!"

"Uh, yeah," I said. "I mean, not that we have to wear the same thing, but . . ." I stopped, not sure how to phrase *I want to look cute too!* without sounding whiny.

"I have an idea," said Amanda, reaching over to pull up the bottom of my tank top.

I stiffened.

"Clemmy, *trust me*," she said, her eyes sparkling.

So I lifted my hands and she looped the bottom of my tank through the neckline, creating a makeshift bikini in one fell swoop. She adjusted it over my bra straps expertly.

I looked down at my chest. *Not bad.*

"Thanks!" I said.

"One more thing." Amanda reached into her bag and brought out a bottle of bright red nail polish called *That Girl.* "I'll do yours first."

With our glossy ruby nails, we sat up on the blanket, peering from behind dark sunglasses and lazing around like we owned the park, giggling at our horoscopes and reading guy advice from *Seventeen* out loud.

And by the end of the afternoon, I felt as cherry-red hot as Amanda did, because she rubbed off on me like that.

chapter three

Day three on the Illinois River. We started out near our house, which is close to Joliet, and now we're heading toward Peoria. I know the route in great detail because Dad has navigation maps all over the place. He's constantly updating us on knot speeds and wind patterns. Thrilling.

My parents are big boat people. Dad was in the navy for a few years after college, and Mom grew up with parents who sailed. They've always had this dream that we'd go live on a sailboat, but they also have jobs and stuff—and Olive and I have school—so it's not like the dream was very realistic. Until my dad, who's a teacher, convinced my mom, who's a lawyer, that she had enough seniority to request a sabbatical this year. Thus, the Great Summer of Boating.

Hoo-ray.

Despite the fact that my mom is officially the first mate of the ship, meaning my dad's right-hand woman, Olive is trying to usurp that role by wearing a silly navy hat and shouting "Aye-aye, Captain!" whenever my dad breathes. I have no interest in participating in the sailing, and I've mostly been down below in my cabin listening to music and itching for an Internet signal. But I know I'd just make myself more unhappy if I could stalk people online and read their "OMG we're having so much fun this summer!!!" updates. It's better to pretend Bishop Heights doesn't exist.

Tonight we're anchored in a tiny inlet off the main river, which is pretty narrow. Olive helps Mom lower the chain, tugging on the anchor to be sure it caught. I sit in the cockpit waiting for dinner—"SpaghettiO Surprise al-fresco," Mom calls it. She brings out bowls of what appears to be a mix of SpaghettiOs and hamburger meat, plus canned peas and sour cream baked together. I'm not saying it's bad, I'm just saying it is definitely from *A Man, A Can, and a Plan*. After we eat, I go to my cabin and continue being a moody loner. It's hard to be antisocial on a forty-two-foot boat, but I'm managing pretty well so far. As long as I eat family dinner with them, my parents mostly leave me alone.

Still, as I hear Mom and Dad and Olive play a game of Triple Solitaire on the fold-up table—laughing and shouting and slapping their hands down on each other's cards—I feel a pang.

I shut off my iPod and listen for a while. At first they're talking about the game. Olive is small, but she has really fast hands.

"No fair!" says Dad. "I couldn't tell if that ace was spades or clubs." He wears thick glasses, so he's always complaining like this and using his eyes as an excuse.

"I'm the only one with just two eyes in this game," says Mom. "And I'm wiping the floor with your combined eight."

Olive stays quiet, but I can almost picture her concentration as she shuffles through the cards in her hands, three at a time, three at a time. She's always got a plan.

Suddenly I hear a wild round of slap-downs, and then a

victorious "I win!" from Olive. "Never count your chickens before the cart, Mom."

I hear my parents crack up—Olive is always mixing two expressions, like "Never count your chickens before they hatch" and "Don't put the cart before the horse." I smile in spite of my perpetual bad mood. But then I hear my sister's feet coming down the hallway toward my door, and I frown again.

She knocks.

"What?" I ask.

"Want to play cards?" She's hanging on the door handle as she peers into my room. I watch her eyes roam around, taking in my scene. iPod at the ready, balled-up tissues on the nightstand, pink feathered pen, and journal open at my side with manic marks in it.

I swat the journal closed in case her glasses are strong enough to let her read from that far away. I've been writing about Ethan again.

"No," I say.

She smiles at me in spite of my negativity. It kind of annoys me, and that makes me feel bad, which makes me more annoyed. Vicious cycle.

"Okay," says Olive gently. "Whenever you're ready."

Then she closes the door softly and goes back to the main cabin.

I hear them shuffle the cards while they talk about me. I don't know why they don't get that we're on a boat where I can hear everything.

"When is she going to snap out of this?" asks Dad.

"She just needs some time," says Mom.

"She's sad," says Olive. And her little voice, so full of sympathy for me even though I've been mean to her, makes fresh tears spring to my eyes.

I feel guilty. I write that down in my journal. Then I curl up in a ball and listen to my family play cards without me.

⛵

The next morning, Dad makes an announcement: we're going to stop at a marina outside of Peoria today for gas and supplies. Our job options are emptying the marine-head holding tank (which is pretty much cleaning the toilet) or going ashore to stock up.

Once it's clear that I'm not going to be able to avoid a task by closing my door and putting in earbuds, I volunteer to go for supplies. The marine toilets completely freak me out.

I take a quick "navy shower" as Dad refers to them—that's where I turn on the water to get wet, turn it off while I soap up and shampoo, then turn it back on to rinse off, so the water's on for, like, a total of one minute, maybe two. Conditioner? It's a luxury of land life.

I'm combing out my wet hair when we pull into the marina. I throw on a white tank top and jean shorts over my bathing suit. Then I slip into my boat shoes, which actually look pretty cool on-boat or off-. They're slate gray with white laces, and they make me feel very nautical.

I grab four canvas eco-bags from the galley cabinet, and Olive meets me in the cockpit. My parents are already hooking up the holding tanks to the marina's waste-suction hose. Dad hands me a few twenties and a list he and Mom made. "See what's available at the dock deli," he says. "They should have most of this stuff."

I nod and start off toward the general store—it's not really called the dock deli, that's just Dad being Dad. I know that Olive's on my heels. I can already feel my legs wobbling; you lose your "land legs" after a few days on the boat, so standing on solid ground again actually feels shaky.

I open the screen door to the store and hold it for Olive. She slips inside and grabs the list from my hands. "I'll get the evaporated milk and the raisins!" she shouts. And then she's off to explore. The store is pretty standard for a marina shop: gray windwashed wood, big live-bait tank with bubbling filters along the wall, a surly bearded guy at the counter with a toothpick in his mouth, just waiting for the boaters to arrive and buy overpriced supplies. There's a poster in the back that makes sexist jokes about why a ship is called "she." One example is "She shows her topsides, hides her bottom, and when coming into port, she always heads for the buoys." Bad puns are really popular with boat people. Just ask the couple docked next to us who named their boat *Knot Shore*.

I pick up a basket and start walking through the aisles, finding Mom's requested chamomile tea (she forgot it) and Dad's giant pack of cinnamon gum (he never brings enough to last more than a few days). As I'm rounding the corner to look for strawberry yogurt, my basket collides directly with someone else's—someone who's filled *his* basket to the brim with bananas. One bunch falls to the ground.

"Oh, crap!" says the redheaded guy attached to the fruit overload.

"Sorry," I say, rubbing my stomach where my own basket jammed into me.

We both lean down to pick up the bananas, and—*boom!*—our foreheads collide.

"Damn!" he says as we stand up. He's holding his head, one eye shut, the other cocked at me, with a big grin on his face.

Then he puts his hands out in front of him, the basket dangling on one arm.

"Okay, back away," he says.

"Huh?" I ask.

"You're obviously an assassin sent to kill me by collision," he says.

I smile slightly and touch my forehead, which is throbbing a little.

"I could say the same thing about you."

Just then, Olive rounds the corner behind the redheaded guy and hits him—*smack!*—in the butt.

"Ooh, sorry!" she says, hurrying past him to get to me. She throws condensed milk into our basket.

"What the—?" says redheaded guy. "Two assassins?!"

I laugh then, and the sound surprises me.

He smiles. "You've got a nice laugh, Miss . . ."

"Williams," I say. "I mean, Clem. I'm Clem."

"I'm James," he says. "It's nice to meet you."

He waves his non-banana-basket-holding hand and I smile. As I may have mentioned, he's got flaming red hair and about a million freckles. He's also supertall and has a grin that engulfs his face. I decide he's cute before I can help myself.

He leans down and successfully picks up the fallen banana bunch.

"Sorry again," I say, edging past him to get to the refrigerated aisle.

"It's quite all right," says James in a game-show-announcer voice. "I'll see you around!"

I keep moving toward the yogurt.

The bell over the door jingles about a minute later, and I imagine Red is gone, back to his boat full of bananas. Which is kind of gross if you think about it, because bananas in tight spaces start to turn and make *everything* smell and taste like banana. Ick.

Olive and I check out a few minutes later, and we walk back to

The Possibility. She chatters on about how she only got the Double Stuf Oreos because Mom said she was allowed to pick one treat that wasn't on the list, and this was like a family pack of treats for us all. I smile at her.

"I support the Double Stuf decision."

"Thanks, Clem!" she shouts, and then she skips ahead, her small body wobbling under the weight of two full canvas grocery bags.

I take my time strolling down the dock to the boat.

There's a tortoiseshell cat stepping along the wooden planks, and I watch her walk toward an old lady who's holding some kind of silver reflecting screen under her chin.

"Ahoy there!" says the lady as I pass. She's got a scratchy voice, like she's smoked for a long time. My grandmother has the same rasp.

"Hello!" I shout, waving my arm in the air to greet her. Boat people tend to be louder and more enthusiastic versions of land people. I guess that's so you can hear and see each other out on the water, and it spills over onto land, too, with real boaters— they're always shouting and gesticulating. This silver-screen lady is no exception.

She puts down her reflecting device and waves me over to her end of the dock. I walk slowly toward her. You can't really ignore boat people. You're not in a hurry to get home, you don't have anything pressing to attend to. You're sailing. It's summer. There are no excuses not to chat.

"Honey, I just love those little sneakers you have on," says the old lady. I notice that her hair is dyed that funny yellow that white-haired people get when they try to stay blond. Her face is sweet-potato orange and her wrinkles are strong and deep, like she's baked for years. I wonder if she's heard about skin cancer and SPF, but I decide it's not my place to tell her.

"Thanks," I say. "I got them in Chicago."

"Oh, city girl?" she says. "I should have known by your walk."

I laugh, for the second time today. "No. Suburban girl. But maybe I'll move to the city one day."

"You should, honey," she says. "That's where adventure lies."

I think that I've had enough adventure for a while, but I don't say that to her. "I'm Clementine."

"Oh my darlin', oh my darlin', oh my darlin' Clementine!" I hear a booming male voice coming from the cabin of sun-lady's boat, and a rounder, more masculine version of the silver-screen lady appears in the cockpit.

"Ahoy there!" he says. This must be their standard greeting.

"Hi," I say, noticing that he's also Oompa Loompa–colored. But his hair is gray and white, not blond. Otherwise, they could be boy-girl twins.

"I'm Ruth, and this is George," says the raspy voice.

"We're doing the Great Loop!" says George. That's what the route we're traveling on is called; it encircles the east coast of the United States and even goes up into Canada, but we're just sailing a small part of it.

"We are too," I say. "Well, not the whole thing. My little sister, Olive, and I have school, and our parents have to go back to work in the fall."

"Don't worry, love," says Ruth. "One day you'll be a retiree like us, and you'll be able to sail all you like!"

"Can't wait," I say, thinking that I will never do another summer like this, stranded with my family and my guilt.

I feel the cat rubbing at my legs.

"Is she yours?" I ask.

"Mrs. Ficklewhiskers." George steps off the boat with a groan. He bends over to scratch her under the chin.

"She's a pirate cat," says Ruth.

"Oh," I say. *Huh?* "Well, I should get these groceries back to my mom."

I turn to walk away, and Ruth says, "Don't lose that stride."

"I won't," I say. "Thanks."

But really? I have no idea what she means. Boat people are often crazy. Did I mention that?

Still, crazy people can be fun—especially during a summer when the sane ones aren't really speaking to you. So I let myself enjoy this moment on land, in the sun.

The redheaded guy was about my age, I think. He didn't look at me like I was a total bitch or some kind of horrible human being. Neither did George or Ruth. They seemed to like me. So did Mrs. Ficklewhiskers, the pirate cat. And I get that that's because they don't know me or what went on with me last year or anything. But still. They all treated me like I had a blank slate. Like I was just plain Clem, a girl with a pretty laugh and a nice walk.

But I guess if they knew me, they'd hate me too.

chapter four

"Ouch!" My elbow slams into the edge of the main cabin doorway as the boat rocks to one side. "Olive, sit down!" I order my sister into a safe spot on the sofa.

I get up to check on Mom and Dad—to see if they need any help above deck. I'm wearing my thick yellow *slicker* (that's what Dad calls it, in a dorky voice), but I still get blasted with sideways rain when I peek my head out of the cabin.

We woke up this morning to a light drizzle. Dad wanted to move anyway—his schedule has us going forty miles today, which will take eight hours at our five-knot speed—and we set out. But we've run into a much bigger storm now that it's early afternoon. We're just looking for shelter.

"Clem, get back down there!" shouts Mom over the howling wind. She's manning the captain's wheel while Dad untangles some ropes near the bow. We hit a wave and my shoulder lurches into the door frame again, but I'm ready this time and I turn so that it doesn't hurt.

I poke my head back out and look forward to make sure Dad's

okay. He waves at me with a big grin on his face. As ridiculous as it sounds, he kind of loves this.

"Okay," I say to Mom. "Call me if you need help."

"Just keep Olive seated."

I go back down and find Olive in the galley, trying to reach the peanut butter.

"Dude, this is not snack time," I say. "Sit. Down."

"I was going to make you something for lunch," says Olive, relenting and walking over to me on experienced sea legs.

"I'm not hungry." Who can eat in this toss-and-turn situation? She's crazy.

We sit together on the couch and I pick up my book, but the words swim in front of me whenever a wave hits, and it makes me feel nauseous. I put the book down.

"Remember when Amanda threw up?" asks Olive. She laughs just like she did that day.

"Yeah," I say, smiling slightly.

It was the summer between seventh and eighth grade, and Amanda and I were on the boat for the weekend with my dad and Olive.

"Do you think each colored chip has a different flavor?" I had asked.

We were waiting for the Funfetti rainbow cake to cool before we frosted it.

"Sure," said Amanda. "Blue is blueberry, pink is strawberry, yellow is banana . . ."

"I don't know." I dipped a spoon into the frosting container and tried to fish out a pink chip. "They all taste kind of vanilla-y to me."

"Have some imagination, Clem," said Amanda, fluttering her electric-blue-mascaraed eyelashes. "It's more fun if they're flavored."

I shrugged. Baking on the boat was this thing Amanda liked to do. "Isn't it crazy that we can make a *cake* while floating at sea?" she'd say. And I'd remind her that we were on a lake, but that didn't seem to matter. Like with the rainbow chip "flavors," boring facts did not deter her colorful worldview.

That day, we had afternoon cake and went for a sail, but it was kind of rough on the water. Not as rough as it is today—not anywhere close—but there were some whitecaps and we rocked a bit as we got out into the big part of the lake.

Olive and I kept trying to convince Amanda that it was best to be above deck when you felt queasy, because seeing stable land and being able to focus on it, unmoving, was the best way to settle your stomach. But she wouldn't come up; she just sat right here on this couch and rocked back and forth. I sat with her and stroked her hair, but I didn't realize how bad she really felt, or I would have gotten her a sick bowl.

Just as Olive came running down to tell us there was calm water ahead, Amanda leaned over to me and vomited right in my lap. She tried to catch it in her hands, and she did get some, but the rest splattered onto my legs. It was my first experience with multicolored vomit.

She looked at me with wide eyes like she thought I was going to get so mad at her—we were always BFFs, but that year, middle school had kind of brought out the mean girls in us, even with each other. Still, how could I do anything but laugh? I jumped up and got a wet towel, and we had the whole thing cleaned up before Dad even noticed. Amanda was mortified. She was sure I'd tell everyone at school or start calling her Rainbow Barf Queen or something.

But Olive and I promised right away that it was our secret, just ours. And I never told anyone. Not even Dad. When he said something smelled funny later, I told him Olive was eating Parmesan cheese that I thought had gone bad. Because Parmesan cheese kind of smells like puke. It's true.

"She was so scared you were going to make fun of her," says Olive, bringing me back to now.

"But I didn't," I say, feeling a sigh coming.

"Of course not!" says Olive. "Because you're the best best friend ever."

I look at my little sister, who doesn't know what she's saying to me, why she's so, so wrong about that.

"I'm not a good friend!" I snap. "And I'm probably not a good sister, either, you should know."

"What are you talking about?" asks Olive, still smiling. She's sure I'm joking—I can see it in her face.

"I'm a terrible, awful friend," I say. "I do horrible things and don't even think about how they'll hurt people."

I stand up and grab my book, needing to get away from Olive, needing my own space. But the boat pitches and I stumble into my sister, almost falling on top of her on the couch.

She grabs my arms. "Clem, why are you so mad?"

"This is the real me," I say. "I'm mean and dark and angry and uncaring."

"No, you're not," she says. I can see annoyance in her eyes now, like this ten-year-old doesn't want to tolerate me. "You're just having a tantrum."

And that makes me so angry that I actually growl at her, if people growl. I make a scary noise—one that I don't even recognize—and I stare at her with hate in my eyes.

Then I push myself up and hurry to my room before another wave hits. I turn on my iPod and close my eyes, feeling the fury of the storm outside echo my internal state. And because I'm dorky,

I think of it as objective correlative, like in English class when the environment is mirroring what the character feels inside. Except this isn't a book—it's my dark and stormy life.

⛵

Later, after the wind has calmed, Olive calls to me in her singsong way to say that there's a rainbow outside. That used to be my favorite thing. We always take a family photo in front of rainbows when we see them, which is a few times a year when we're out on the boat.

But I don't answer Olive. I don't move. And she doesn't call to me twice.

chapter five

By the time we sail into the next marina, I've done something awful.

I looked at the photos on my phone.

Back when I was happy with my life, like, two weeks ago, I used to take a candid shot every day, just to chronicle daily existence, I guess. I almost put them on Tumblr, but I decided to keep them for myself—thank goodness. At least 50 percent of the shots from this spring capture moments I wish I could forget.

I don't know why I did this. Maybe because I'm bored out here, with nothing to do but read and watch DVDs on a tiny TV and sit on the bow while we bob along across the water. Maybe because I enjoy making myself feel like crap. A little self-flagellation is healthy, right?

Or maybe it's because I've had all this reflecting time, and I started thinking about the redheaded guy and how I felt really nice when he talked to me in the store. At first I imagined he could somehow see my true self. He could tell that I wasn't a bad person. It felt like a Band-Aid on my broken heart.

But then I realized that was dumb.

He doesn't know me at all. He thought I was kind of cute, but he probably hadn't seen a girl his age in weeks. There aren't that many sixteen-year-old boaters out here. Red is not a redeemer come to tell the world that I'm not so bad, really. If he got to know me, he would think I'm a terrible person too. After all, if my best friend in the world—after years of knowing me—can cast me off like she has, then this stranger certainly isn't going to like me. At least, he wouldn't if he got to know me.

And that's how my self-hating voices go. They also like to look at last year's photos and feel nostalgic for something that never should have been. It's how they roll.

Damn voices.

We tie up at EastPort Marina in Peoria, and my dad wants me and Olive to come with him to get some live bait for fishing. Olive's been excited about throwing a line in, but we haven't done it yet because Dad really wanted to get to our first big destination. No, Peoria isn't big. But it counts when you're boating this super-rural route.

There's a dock deli here, too—there is at most marinas, I'm learning—and Dad and Olive pick out some creepy-crawlies while I stand back and mope. It's what I'm good at these days. I'm trying not to resist my parents' requests (to eat meals with them, to help bring in the sails at night when we dock, to remind Olive that being first mate doesn't always mean she gets to drop the anchor—especially if we're near a strong current), but I have trouble showing any enthusiasm. I'm tired a lot too. It's exhausting being sad.

Today is incredibly hot, especially for June in Illinois, when it's usually in the eighties. It has to be at least ninety-five degrees out. As we walk back to *The Possibility*, Olive declares: "I'm going swimming!"

Then she looks up at me. "Are you?"

And maybe it's the heat, or maybe it's my little sister's hopeful eyes, but for some reason I say yes.

Twenty minutes later, the swimming idea has grown into a full-on recreation day. Mom and Olive are packing up a picnic lunch to take in the dinghy—a tiny little boat called *Sea Ya* (ha-ha) that we can just squeeze into to go island hopping off *The Possibility*—and I'm wearing my red swimsuit. My room is giving me cabin fever. It'll be good to get outside.

We load up the cooler, fishing poles, a tackle box, towels, and sunscreen. That's pretty much all we need. I sit up front with Olive while Mom leans against Dad in the back. We motor over to a sandy shore just around the bend from the marina, and Olive drops the little anchor. I swing a leg over the side to check the depth. The chilly water feels like icy relief on my legs. My feet hit the muddy bottom and the water's only up to my waist, so Mom hands me the cooler and I walk it over to land. Mom and Olive follow with towels while Dad tinkers with the fishing rods.

And you know what happens next? We have a really nice day. One of those family days that makes you think you could be in the part of the movie with the musical interlude. We eat peanut butter and jelly sandwiches, we swim and reapply sunscreen on each other, Dad chases Mom with a washed-up fish head on a stick, and I even laugh out loud. Twice!

As the sun starts to lower in the sky, Dad and Olive take the dinghy out a little deeper so they can do some fishing while Mom and I walk along the shore. We're on a mission to find a single shell worthy of the jar she keeps secured on a shelf in the main cabin of the boat. She grew up sailing near her home on the North Carolina seashore, so the jar is full of shells from her past— lots from boating trips with my grandparents, some from our own family voyages. There's one from her high school prom date, who gave her a shell on a string in lieu of a corsage because he knew it was more her style. And there's one from the beach in Martha's Vineyard where she went with her grandmother after high school graduation. They're not all perfect or pretty, but each one has a story. And she thinks today is special enough to be remembered. I guess I do too.

I find an opened black mussel shell with two sides still joined together. It looks like a lopsided heart, and I hold it for her to see. She comes over and peers into my hand.

"Perfect," she says. "You've got a good eye."

"At least that makes two of us in this family," I say, and Mom throws her head back to laugh. It wasn't *that* funny, but she and I are secretly proud to have 20/20 vision, unlike Dad and Olive, and I know she appreciates me making my first attempt at humor in about three weeks.

"Here," I say, handing the shell over to her. She palms it carefully and slips it into the pocket of her cotton shirt.

We start back down the beach, and I look out at the water to see Olive pulling in a little sunfish. I smile.

"Clem?" says Mom, and my heart sinks. I can already tell she's going to ask me about Amanda. She's got this tone. It almost sounds like *she* might cry when she uses it, and I recognize it instantly.

"Mom?" I respond, annoyed, already getting defensive. I was having such a nice day.

"Have you thought about maybe writing Amanda a letter?" she asks. "Just putting everything out there . . . explaining . . ."

"Explaining what?" I ask. "Explaining that I suck, I'm selfish, and I'm obviously a bad person who doesn't deserve her friendship?"

I take a breath.

"Is that what I should *explain*, Mom?"

"No," says Mom. Then she looks away from me and out to the water. "Well, maybe Amanda . . ."

"Amanda and I are not friends anymore," I say, quietly now, as I struggle to swallow tears.

"But if you tried to tell her . . . ," says Mom.

"Just shut up about it!" I scream. Dad and Olive hear me and turn in our direction, but Mom waves at them so they won't worry.

"I guess you're not ready yet, then," she says, under her breath.

I hate it when parents say stuff like that, because it's like they think you'll eventually reach some unchartable point of emotional maturity when you *will* be ready to do something the way they think it should be done—writing this cure-all letter, for example. But the truth is, a letter to Amanda is a stupid idea. And besides, it's not like I didn't think of that. I've been trying to write one every night for three weeks, but when I reread my drafts I just hear how whiny I sound. It's pathetic. I can't make the words mean anything.

I sit down in the sand for a minute, just to catch my breath. I still feel like there's a lead weight on my chest every time I think about last year. Can't Mom see that I *don't want to talk about it*?

"Oh, honey." Mom sits beside me and rubs my back, making gentle circles with her fingers just like she did when I was little and couldn't sleep. I start to calm down, slowly.

"Mom, can we just leave it alone?"

She stays quiet.

"And another thing," I say. "I'm avoiding guys. Forever."

"Forever?" she asks.

"Well, forever this summer, anyway."

"Okay," she says quietly. "I'm sorry I said anything."

"Fine." I'm still bothered, but I try to shake off the mood that overtook me so quickly.

"Really," says Mom. "Let's drop it." She's smiling and acting like herself again. "Today isn't the day."

"Good," I say.

"But I do have one more question." I look up at her and see that she's wearing that young-looking smile again, the one that means she's about to make fun of me.

"What?" I ask.

"Is this 'no guys this summer' thing why you aren't waving back to that boy from the EastPort Marina over there?"

I look out and see the redheaded guy on a boat called *Dreaming of Sylvia*. He's obviously the first mate for his father, or whoever the older guy at the captain's wheel is. Red is unfurling the jib, and in between rope pulls, he's waving in our direction. They're out in the river beyond Dad and Olive, passing by and not coming into our inlet, but I can clearly make out his fiery hair.

"How do you know he was at EastPort?" I ask, wondering if Mom was spying on me when I had my run-in with Red.

"I talked to his father there," says Mom. "They're from Turnerville. They're making the same Great Loop we are."

Mom waves back, and so do Dad and Olive, but I don't.

Now that I know we're on a parallel route—and that he's from Turnerville, which is, like, forty minutes away from Bishop Heights—I definitely don't want to encourage more interaction. Red met me; he likes me. And in order to keep things that way, I'm going to stay as far away from him as possible.

chapter six

Dear Amanda,
I wish I could tell you about the summer so
far. Olive is being clingy. Dad is being cheesy.
Mom is being nosy (about us and our fight).
I wish . . .

Rip. Another page for the trashed-letters drawer.

⛵

It's not like we were each other's only friends. There were a group
of us—me, Amanda, Henry Choi, Aaron Blake, and Renee Hart-
well. Amanda and I were like the core, somehow, always tighter
than the friends floating around us, but the five of us definitely
had a unit.

"The lighting isn't working," said Henry, staring at Renee
pointedly. "Amanda looks splotchy."

"Maybe Amanda *is* splotchy," said Aaron, raising his eyebrows
in a mock-serious gesture.

"Shut up!" Amanda threw a small couch pillow at him.

"Excellent use of the 'throw pillow,'" I said, using air quotes to emphasize my joke.

Aaron cracked up. Amanda smiled.

Henry frowned. "Renee, fix the lighting?" he said.

Renee shifted her weight, struggling to move the spotlight while also holding up the giant microphone rig that was her charge during this student-film experiment.

Henry really wanted to go to a film school program in California over the summer, and he had to turn in a three-minute short with his application. We all agreed to help him shoot it over an early fall weekend, but I think Renee was less than thrilled with her role, which included major behind-the-scenes physical labor.

She's the tomboy type—always wearing jeans or shorts and a T-shirt, hair in a ponytail, very casual. I thought that was cool about her, the way she didn't chase guys. But that didn't mean she didn't have her eye on someone; it was clear to everyone who looked twice that she totally loved Henry. You don't work hot lights and hold a heavy microphone boom on a Saturday for just anyone.

Amanda and I were cast as two women in our early forties dealing with infertility, who meet in the waiting room of our mutual doctor, played by Aaron.

"Remind me again why we have to be forty-somethings," I said, wiping at the brown makeup that was supposed to make my face look shadowy and older.

Henry shaped his hands into a rectangle and looked at me with one eye closed. He was always doing things like that, which I think he saw in the movies, ironically. I'm not sure he even knew *why* film people did that.

"Everyone and their sister is going to turn in movies about coming-of-age and young love and blah, blah, blah CW crap," he said. "But *I* am going to turn in a thoughtful exploration of middle age."

"Is this because your parents have been watching DVDs of that old show *thirtysomething*?" asked Amanda.

Henry sighed. "It's a good show."

Amanda and I looked at each other and started laughing.

"Can we get this scene done, please?" Henry sounded like he was about to lose it, so we settled down.

He didn't have one of those official black-and-white clapboard things that you crack, so when we all got back to our places, Henry just yelled, "Action!" from behind the camera.

"I haven't tried intravenous yet," said Amanda in a very serious voice, leaning in to me conspiratorially.

I looked at her and burst out laughing again.

"In-vitro!" shouted Henry. "It's called *in-vitro* fertilization."

"She could just say IVF," said Renee. "That's what my mom's friend kept calling it."

"Fine, IVF," said Henry. "Okay, let's start again."

We ran the scene six more times until Henry was satisfied that he had the right pieces to cut together. Then we had to film it from another angle. It was a long day, but a really fun one, and I remember looking around and thinking it felt like being with family.

⛵

After everything happened, it wasn't like Renee and Aaron and Henry vandalized my locker or threw eggs at me or anything dramatic like that. They just, kinda . . . weren't there. Renee sent me a message saying she needed to "figure things out," which I guess meant she wasn't ready to talk to me. Henry and Aaron asked if

I was okay at school, but they didn't, like, make any real effort to make sure that when I said "Yeah," I was telling the truth.

And, honestly, I had tunnel vision: all that mattered was Amanda. And of course, it was natural that everyone sided with her. I was the one who did something wrong.

chapter seven

"Another one!" Dad whisper-shouts, pointing toward the dark night sky.

He and I are in the cockpit, each stretched out on a cushioned seat, looking straight up at the stars. Mom and Olive have gone to bed—they're the morning people on this vessel. Dad, a night owl like me, heard about a meteor shower tonight, and we've been hanging out here for half an hour or so, watching shooting stars. I've seen six and Dad claims to have seen eleven—twelve counting this latest one, which I didn't catch. I think that's impossible.

"Your eyes are playing tricks on you, old man," I tell him.

He laughs. "Maybe so." I look in his direction and I can see his white hair ruffling in the breeze. Mom's freckles make her look young, but Dad's prematurely white hair—not to mention his round belly—sometimes makes him look like Santa Claus with nerd glasses. He used to be blond, but that was before my time. I used to wish my hair were white when I was younger—I thought it was so unique. Even luminous, somehow.

I look up again. The sky is huge out here on the water. It's so big you can see the curve of the earth, which makes me a little dizzy. Sometimes the sky freaks me out, to be honest. Space and the universe and all that? Scary.

We settle back into a comfortable quiet, and I'm thinking about how nice it is that Dad and I can do this—sit out here and be silent together. Mom's always talking or bringing something up, but Dad's more relaxed, more . . .

He clears his throat, which puts me on edge instantly. Dad never clears his throat unless he's nervous about something.

"So do you miss them?" Dad asks.

"Sorry?"

"Amanda, Aaron, Ethan, your friends . . . ," says Dad.

I close my eyes and shake my head. Just when I thought Dad was being cool, he has to go and bring this up. I didn't even know he knew Ethan's name. I wish he didn't.

"Did Mom ask you to talk to me about this?"

"No," says Dad. "I just know something's been on your mind, and I thought you might like to let some of it out."

I hate that my parents assume they know what I'm thinking about when I close myself up in my room. They always imagine that they understand situations so much better than I do, but do they know Ethan? No. They've never even met him—they just saw him in a Facebook photo one night when Amanda and I were on the computer in the den, and Mom asked Amanda which guy her boyfriend was. They don't even know Amanda, really—not like I do. Mom thinks she's a saint because she does things like make emergency cupcakes for the church bake sale on just a day's notice. They have no idea she actually bought them at a bakery outside of town and then smudged up the frosting a little to make them look homemade.

"No," I lie. "I don't miss him—er, them."

"It's okay to miss him, you know," says Dad. So maybe he

knows more than I thought he did. And I'm glad that we're both looking up and not facing each other right now, because a tear slides down my cheek before I can stop it.

It's not like the tear is all sadness. The thought of Ethan still affects me—I feel sad, mad, nostalgic, bitter, excited, wistful, energized, and, like, a hundred other emotions whenever he enters my mind. Also, I've done something ridiculous. I've gone through my iPod and found all the songs Ethan put on my playlist—well, all the ones I still had on there, anyway—and then recreated it as an on-the-go situation. I am completely masochistic.

"He isn't mine to miss," I say a minute later, after I control the quiver I know would have crept into my voice if I'd responded right away.

"No one belongs to anyone, Clem. Especially not when you're sixteen years old."

"Dad, let's just say there are rules."

"I know," says my dad. "I know all about the rules. There are times when life gets lived outside the rules, though."

"Yeah, well, high school is pretty unforgiving of social rule-breakers," I say. "Believe me, my ex-friends have made that very clear."

"Well, maybe that says more about your friends than it does about you," says Dad.

I know he's trying to help with his circular vagueness, but I'm so not in the mood. He doesn't know the details, and I'm not about to try to explain everything to him. It's like I'm inside this situation that has so many different emotional components and friend connections that it feels like a web that only I and maybe, like, two other people can totally grasp. I decide that I'm staying quiet, looking for one more shooting star, and then going to bed. That way it won't seem like I left because of this conversation.

A few seconds later, I see a bright light streak across the starboard side of the sky.

"Whoa," I say.

"That was a big one," says Dad. "I hope you made a wish."

"I did."

I stand up and kiss him on the forehead.

"Good night, Dad."

"Good night, Curious Clem," he says.

He used to call me that when I was little. I'd ask him a million questions about everything—the boat, his shirt buttons, the color of the sky. Anything that entered my field of vision, really. I've lost some of that curious nature, though. I have answers now, and they're not all as magical or interesting as I once thought they would be.

When I tuck into my bed, I try to think, from a curious perspective, about Dad's question: *Do I miss Ethan?* I miss my friends, I miss the way my life was before Ethan was around, and—okay—I miss the way I felt when I was with Ethan.

And I wonder if it makes me a bad person.

chapter eight

Dear Amanda,
I always envied the way you were with guys.
It was like you could cast a spell on them or
something...

"So that new kid Ethan is in my Physics class," she said.

"Oh, he's in my AP American History."

At my house after school in early September, we sat on my bed and stared into the mirror. I had a brush in my hand and was slowly combing through my long brown hair. Amanda was trying on different lipsticks with a box of tissues by her side.

"He's a junior, so he could technically go off campus, but I'm thinking about inviting him to sit with us at lunch." She pursed her lips and applied a dark pink that made her pale skin look luminous.

"That looks so much better on you," I said. "Take it."

She smiled. "Really?"

I nodded.

"I can trade you for the cheek stain I got at Sephora last week."

"Deal."

She reached into her bag and pulled out a thick, sparkly pink pencil. "You can use it on your lips too."

"Thanks."

"I think he's from Ohio or something. So do you think he's cool?" she asked.

"Who?"

"That kid, Ethan."

"Oh," I said, making pink circles on the apples of my cheeks like they do in the commercials. Ethan Garrison. I didn't think much of him. He was tall and sort of goofy looking, with floppy brown hair that was too long to be short and neat, but not long enough to be, like, intentionally long hair. It was *unkempt*. That's the word that came to mind when he walked into my AP American History class on the first day of school and sat across the room from me. "Yeah, he seems nice."

Amanda smiled then, and I saw its meaning, even in the mirror. It meant that Ethan had become more than the new kid—he was now Soon-to-Be Amanda's Boyfriend.

She always had a boyfriend. Amanda had dated Daniel Bick and Rob Morris and Seth Hirschberg—each for three months plus. She's the kind of girl who knows how to smile at a guy, what to say to make him feel good, how to throw her head back ever so slightly when she laughs to show off her long, elegant neck. She's gorgeous, too, but not in an obvious way. She has really short blond hair—a pixie cut that might look boyish or mom-like on someone else, but there's something about her face. Her eyes are huge and open, almost, like, anime-sized. And they're always full of light, a little joyful, a little teasing.

And now that I knew she had her sights set on Ethan, it was my job to be encouraging.

"He's really funny in history," I said. It was true. I had a positive feeling about him, like he was a nice guy who'd be good for my friend.

Amanda flopped down on the bed dramatically. "So we should study, right?"

She never spent long talking about guys—she wasn't into that. She just established her interest and moved on.

"Yeah." I sighed and pulled out my Honors English vocab sheet. We had this really hard teacher who drilled us on SAT words every week. The year before, two kids in her class got perfect verbal scores, so I guess her methods worked, but still—exhausting.

"Let me quiz you," said Amanda.

I gave her my worksheet and rested my back against the wall. She stretched out on my pillow and put her legs across my lap.

"Celerity."

I rolled my eyes. "Start with one I know!"

"That's not any fun," she said, smiling.

"I truly have zero idea," I said. "I haven't started studying these yet."

"Okay, think of it this way: if you drank celery tea, it would probably just run straight through you."

"You mean I'd have to pee?"

"Yes, and you'd have to rush to find a bathroom with *swiftness* and *speed*," Amanda said with a grin. "Good, right?"

"I'm supposed to see the word *celerity* on a test and think of drinking celery tea—which I'm not even sure is a real thing—and having to run to the bathroom?"

"Yes!" She was superpleased with herself. "It'll work. Trust me."

We went through the rest of the list, and Amanda thought up

silly memory devices for each one. *Capricious*: "Think of me! I'm a Capricorn and I am so *fickle* with guys." *Wanton*: "This is how you act around Chinese food like wonton soup—totally *lustful* and *undisciplined*."

Some of her ideas were a real stretch, but I spent the whole study session laughing.

"We're so acing this test," she said when she was packing up to go home.

"Obviously, because we're geniuses."

"Naturally."

She gave me a small wave and an excited smile as she left my room. "Ethan tomorrow!" she said.

And I knew he'd be hers. Who could resist Amanda?

chapter nine

The first time I really noticed Ethan was when our history teacher, Mr. King, made an incredibly lame joke. I rolled my eyes, and then saw Ethan see me do it. He smiled. I smiled back. His smile? It was nice. But it wasn't like I was hit by lightning or anything.

The second week of school, Amanda invited him to eat lunch with us for the first time. Henry, Aaron, Renee, Amanda, and I always had this one picnic table on the quad—we'd kind of claimed it freshman year. Amanda and I even carved our initials on the top right corner of the table: CLEMANDA = BFF.

When Ethan came over to sit, Amanda patted the space next to her, and he and I ended up across from each other. Everyone made awkward small talk with Ethan; it was horribly dull, so I said, "Enough small talk."

And he said, "This isn't small talk. This is *enormous* talk." It's a line from this old movie called *Frankie and Johnny* that my parents love.

So I snorted Dr Pepper through my nose. For real.

"Yes!" Ethan did a fist pump. "I got Clementine Williams to laugh."

"Like that's some big feat?" I challenged, feeling pretty flattered that he knew my full name; it was early in the year and we hadn't even really talked to each other yet.

"You only break at the truly funny stuff," he said. "I've noticed in history."

Then he popped a Dorito in his mouth and grinned at Amanda.

"It's true," she said. "Clem has a totally selective funny bone."

"Just because I don't laugh at the preview parts of movies like *some* people," I said.

"Ugh, I hate that!" said Ethan, crumpling his Dorito bag in disgust. "Could people's humor be more generic?"

I looked pointedly at Amanda then, and she giggled as she raised her hand. "Guilty," she said. "Those are the best parts!" Her voice came out all cute, and I saw Ethan melt.

That was the predictable moment of the day—guys always turned to goo for Amanda. But the amazing thing was, Ethan made me laugh extra hard, like, ten more times that afternoon.

As we walked to Mr. King's history class together after lunch, we saw this kid in our grade named Kevin in the hall.

"Is it me, or does he look exactly like a young version of Mr. King?" Ethan whispered out of the side of his mouth.

I glanced at Kevin. "Completely."

"YMK!" Ethan shouted at Kevin as we passed. He held up his hand for a high five, and inexplicably, Kevin smacked it.

"Hey, man," Kevin said, as if Ethan shouting "YMK" at him made any sense at all.

"Young Mr. King," Ethan whispered after Kevin was gone.

"I got it," I said, my hand clapped over my mouth to stop the laughs.

"And *that* is why I like you," said Ethan.

In class, our desks were in this U shape that Mr. King liked to say promoted discussion, and Ethan's seat was right across from mine. We had just sat down when Sharon Golding walked in wearing sunglasses *over* her regular glasses. I glanced at Ethan with my *WTF?* face, and he mouthed "Six eyes?" I cracked up, but no one else even noticed.

Later when Mr. King called on me to talk about the causes of the Civil War, I answered with a smartass quote from *The Simpsons*, and Ethan let out a big guffaw.

It was like he and I shared this connection. We'd look over at each other and start laughing at least three times per class. After a few weeks Mr. King even said, "Clem and Ethan—if you were sitting together, I'd threaten to separate you. As it is, I'll ask you to avoid flirtatious glances while I'm teaching."

That made us laugh even harder. We weren't flirting, we were just sort of becoming good friends. And it was great to be good friends with your best friend's boyfriend, right?

chapter ten

We pull into the Grafton Harbor Marina in Grafton, Illinois, where the Illinois River meets the Mississippi. There's a sign that says THE KEY WEST OF THE MIDWEST, and there appears to be a floating booze cruise nearby. This is not the place we should be right now.

I won't go into great detail, but it seems that sometime in the night, our toilet clogged. *Ours* meaning mine and Olive's.

"I think somebody had one too many Double Stuf Oreos last night," I say at breakfast.

Olive scowls at me, but there's no avoiding it. This morning, our family was faced with a foul, odorous reality. That's why we're all above deck now as Dad pulls alongside the dock—it is *way* stinky down below. I jump off the boat and tie us off.

An appreciative whistle echoes behind me.

"Nice cleat knot," says Red. I recognize his voice before I see him. When I do turn around, I notice that his orange hair is tucked into a Boston Red Sox baseball cap. He looks cute. I smile at him.

"Thanks."

Then I see his face contort. The smell from the head has hit him.

If this weren't so hilarious, I'd be mortified. As it stands, though, I have to laugh.

Just then, Olive steps off the boat.

I look at her, then back at Red, raising my eyebrows.

"No way," he whispers.

I nod. I feel bad selling out my own sister, but I can't have him associating this awful smell with me for the rest of the summer.

Olive marches down the dock past Red like she hasn't a care in the world. She holds her head a little too high, though, and I know she's embarrassed.

I turn back to Red and remember that I really don't want to talk to him any more than necessary.

"I should go—" I start, trying to get past him.

He lets me by, but then he follows me at a quick clip, keeping up with my long strides.

"Did you need something?" I ask him, when it's clear that he's not going off in his own direction.

"No," he says.

I keep walking. He stays with me step for step.

"Well, yeah," he continues. "I've been meaning to tell you something."

"What?" I ask, more like *What? You've been thinking about the fact that you need to tell me something after you met me once for thirty seconds?* than *What have you been meaning to tell me?* But he takes it the second way.

"It's about the bananas," he says.

"The bananas . . ." I slow down my walk to a normal stroll.

"Yeah," he says. "There were a ton in my cart the other day, and I didn't want you to get the wrong idea."

"*Okaaay . . .*"

"I mean, you know, bananas are, like, the *worst* thing to have in closed spaces because they can really stink up the joint after a few days with that rotten-banana smell," he says. "And it's not like I'm Betty Crocker or something and planning to make banana bread when they start to turn. I mean, I'm kind of impressed with myself that I even know that you can do that with brown bananas, but just because I know you *can* do it doesn't mean I'm capable of the actual execution of baking banana bread."

"Uh-huh," I say, barely keeping up with his verbal flow.

"But I wanted you to know that I'm not one of those people who lets bananas stink up the boat," he says. "It's just that my dad likes to have about five bananas a day—the man is like Mr. Chiquita over there, so we have to keep them stocked. It's almost like he's a banana chain-smoker."

Then he chuckles to himself and takes a tiny notebook from his back pocket. He flips it open.

He stops walking, and so do I.

He writes something down, shuts the notebook, then looks up and sees my confusion.

"Oh." He opens it again and shows me what he wrote.

Dad smokes a banana.

I stay silent.

"I like to draw," says Red. "The image of my dad smoking a banana is one I want to capture at some point, so I have to remember it. Don't worry, I'll write 'Inspired by Clem' on the back so I won't forget who gave me the idea."

"I didn't give you the idea," I say, kind of impressed that he remembers my name. *What was his real name again? Josh? Joe? John?*

"Well, not directly, but definitely indirectly," says Red. "I wouldn't have thought of it if I hadn't been explaining to you that I'm not one of those people who has bananas everywhere that go brown. We don't let them go brown. My dad eats them too fast!"

He pauses and I just stare at him.

"So, yeah," he says, finally letting the awkwardness of this entire encounter wash over him for a moment. But just a moment. Then he smiles like we're old friends. "That's what I wanted to tell you."

"Uh . . . thanks." I hide my grin because I don't want to encourage Red, but I'm a little bit happy he told me, because I did have that thought about the bananas. And most people don't think like I do. Only Amanda really. And Ethan.

"Do you remember my name, Clem?" he asks me suddenly.

"Of course." I'm internally panicking but externally acting quite cool, I think.

He folds his arms across his chest and blocks the narrow bridge to land.

"What is it?"

"Well, I might not remember your actual name," I say. "But the thing is, I gave you a nickname."

His eyes widen in delight, but they're tinged with suspicion, if I read him correctly. Which I think I do. This guy is like an open book. "Really?" he asks. "Tell me."

And here's where I don't want to admit that my nickname is so obvious and lame. I quickly scan my brain—which I usually think of as a very sharp tool—and try to come up with a fake nickname. I can't tell him that I've been thinking of him as "Red."

"Please don't say Carrot-Top or something awful like that," he says, before I can answer. "Carrot tops are green, anyway."

He does have a point there.

I'm still silent while he keeps going: "What is it, like, 'Mr. Universe'? Or 'That-Really-Smart-and-Funny-Guy'?"

Okay, as fast as my mind is, Red's is faster. I'm totally pressured, and I cave.

"I was calling you Red in my head," I say.

So lame.

"Hmm . . . original," he says, but he's smiling. "It's James. James Townsend. You could go with JT, or just call me James, or even Red, if you must, though I prefer Burnt Sienna."

I can feel my face turning burnt sienna.

"Cle-em!" shouts Olive. She's peeking her head out of the dock deli and waving to me. "I need some money!"

"I've got to, um . . . ," I start.

He gets out of my way this time.

"As long as we're clear on the state of me and bananas," he says.

"Clear," I say, willing myself to remember *James.*

Then I walk up the dock and don't turn around to see if James is watching me. But I think he is.

⛵

My family spends the rest of the day cleaning—Mom says the boat needs a good once-over anyway. I'm pretty sure she says that so Olive doesn't have to feel too bad about the toilet issue taking up a whole day of our trip, but it's nice of her.

James is over on his boat, *Dreaming of Sylvia*, and he waves to me every now and then. They're just across the water from us on Pier 2. I guess I don't see the harm in being friendly; it's not as though we're going to be hanging out for more than, like, five minutes at a dock if our boats happen to be in the same spot at the same time.

The cleanup takes longer than I thought it would, and soon Dad has adjusted to the idea that we'll stay at the marina overnight—the dockmaster found a slip for us.

Around five o'clock, the sun is right in my eyes, but when I shade them with my hand I see James's dad striding down their pier. I watch him walk across the land to our pier and head toward *The Possibility*.

"I'm Bill Townsend," he says when he reaches me. I'm the only one outside at the moment.

"Clem Williams."

"I met your folks the other night," says Bill. "And I hear you've met my son, James."

"I have," I say. "I hear you like bananas."

I don't know why I say that—it just comes out. Bill smiles, though. "I do," he says.

Then he continues, "Well, now that we've got the formalities of names and bananas straightened out, I'd like to invite you and your parents and your sister to join us on *Dreaming of Sylvia* for dinner."

My head whips up before I can stop it. "Dinner?" I ask stupidly.

"That's right."

"Tonight?"

Man, I sound like a total idiot.

"No time like the present!" says Bill, laughing at me a little.

Just then, Dad comes out of the cockpit and saves me. He and Bill shake hands and proceed to make plans for this dinner date. I keep hosing off the side of the boat absentmindedly, eavesdropping on them.

When Bill leaves, Dad says, "Well, that was nice." Then he goes down below to tell Mom.

I lean against the side of *The Possibility* and look back toward the Townsends' boat. James isn't outside at the moment, and I wonder briefly if he sent his father over, if this was his idea.

I fold my arms across my chest and resolve to be cordial, but not overly friendly, at dinner.

This is the Summer of Me, when I figure out who I am and who my friends are and how to fix the things that happened last year. I'm not one of those girls who finds a guy and gets happy. Besides, with my track record, James is probably someone's boy-friend anyway.

As nice as it is to talk to someone my own age, someone who makes me laugh, even, I am still in self-punishing mode. And all I see is dumb distraction with James. Dumb distraction and a so-cute smile. Ack.

chapter eleven

Dear Amanda,
Sometimes it seemed like you were hiding
things from me too. Like you didn't tell me
everything anymore...

⛵

"Ethan's boxers, holiday themed?" I said. "That's not a fair item."

"Everything's fair," said Amanda. "I didn't make the list—Henry did."

Henry loved creating scavenger hunts for us to do on the weekends. Bishop Heights is a small town, so creative minds tend to run our lives, and Henry was definitely our most adventurous and inventive friend.

"How does Henry even know that Ethan has holiday-themed boxers?" asked Renee.

"He does," said Amanda. "I can vouch." She was sitting on the army-green shag carpet in Henry's basement, fingering the edges of her favorite sparkly blue ballet flats. Amanda was good at being coy.

"So are you guys officially dating?" Renee leaned forward and stared at Amanda intensely, and I was glad she was asking point-blank. I'd asked the week before, but Amanda just confessed to a kiss in the parking lot—she wouldn't use the word *boyfriend*. Yet.

"Maybe," said Amanda, her grin growing.

"So why isn't Ethan here?" I asked.

"I invited him, but his grandparents are in town." Amanda stuck out her lips in a pout. "His mom insisted on a family night."

"Good," said Aaron. "One more would have thrown off team numbers."

The teams were me and Aaron versus Renee and Amanda—mainly because Aaron and Renee both had early fall birthdays and already had their licenses—with Henry acting as Director of Scavenge and Official Point Tallier. The list looked like this:

EASY (1 point):
1 tip cup from Ben & Jerry's, minus the tips
1 bag of orange candy circus peanuts—extra points
  for eating them upon reconvening
1 official traffic cone

MEDIUM (2 points):
1 buoy from Dilby Lake
1 size-6 vintage shoe (ladies)
1 pair of Ethan's boxers (holiday themed)

HARD (3 points):
1 signed note from Henry's mom saying she'll allow him
  to stay out all night for prom

1 family portrait from Principal Sullivan's house
1 (used) hairnet from a Wendy's employee (with
  signature on a napkin attesting to its authenticity)

No team could get everything on the list in our two-hour time frame, obviously, but the idea was to get at least one Hard-level thing, because they were worth the most points. If you went for all Easy stuff, you'd never be able to win.

"I think we should beat Amanda to Ethan," I said as soon as Aaron and I got in his car. He has a speedy little Jeep that he always drives for scavenger hunts because it has an obnoxious horn honk—it plays "La Cucaracha"—and he likes to tease the other team with it.

"It would definitely make her mad . . . ," said Aaron, smirking. "Let's do it!" Then he peeled out of Henry's gravel driveway, spraying some rocks for effect. He hit the horn, too, a signal that the hunt was *on*.

We sped to Ethan's house. Amanda's car was nowhere in sight—she and Renee must have gone after something else.

"I'll go." I bolted from the passenger seat and ran up to Ethan's front door.

I knocked three times. I was already laughing in anticipation when Ethan opened the door. He smiled this huge smile.

"Clem!" he said. "I thought you guys were—"

His gaze went to Aaron's car behind me.

"Uh-oh . . . *I'm* not on the scavenger hunt list, am I?"

"Nope," I said. "But your boxers are! Holiday themed, specifically."

"Ethan, who's at the—?" Ethan's mom appeared behind him. "Well, is this Amanda? She's even prettier than you said!"

57

I turned red instantly. *Please let her not have heard me say boxers.*

"No, this is Clem," said Ethan. "She's a friend of Amanda's. I mean, she's my friend too. She's . . . Clem."

He looked so cute as he got flustered in front of his mom.

"Hi, Mrs. Garrison," I said, smiling in what I hoped was an innocent-and-winning way.

"Won't you come in, Clem . . . Clementine, is it?" she asked. "Such a lovely name."

"Um, yeah, thanks," I said, glancing back at Aaron, who was gesturing wildly, urging me to come back to the car, to abandon the mission. We were losing time and had to keep going, but I wasn't going to give up on this one. I gave him a palm that meant "Wait," and I headed into Ethan's house.

Once inside, Ethan disappeared while I met his dad, his grandparents, and a visiting uncle. It was like a family reunion.

Just as Grandpa Garrison was launching into a round of "Oh my darlin', oh my darlin' . . ." and I was thinking I was going to face an epic fail on the underwear quest, Ethan saved me.

"Clem needs to pick up this stuff for history class," he said, thrusting a thick red three-ring binder into my hands. "She has a big project due, so she has to get going, but I'm sure you'll meet her again another time."

He looked over at me and smiled. "She's one of my best friends at school."

I felt my heart pitter-patter then, and in a burst of energy I stood on my tiptoes and hugged him quickly before I headed for the front door, calling "Good night, everyone!" as Grandpa Garrison kept humming my namesake song.

When I got back to the car I was holding the binder to my

chest. I jumped in and held it up to show Aaron, who was shouting that I'd taken *forever*.

"Score!" I said, opening up the binder. Inside was a pair of red boxers with candy canes all over them, and a Post-it from Ethan.

That silenced the shouting.

"Nice!" said Aaron.

He pulled out of the driveway and headed for Ben & Jerry's as I looked at the note.

"C, I certify that these are mine," I read out loud. "Please return them soon. Heart, E."

"Heart?" asked Aaron. "He wrote H-E-A-R-T on there?"

"No, he drew a heart," I said.

"I think you read that as *love*," he said. "Because obviously he loves you."

"Totally." I knew Aaron was joking, but I still felt excited about that heart. I stuffed the note in my pocket.

When we returned to Henry's house at the end of the night, we'd managed to get six of the nine items on the scavenger hunt list. We presented each thing one by one as Henry diligently tallied the score on his official scavenger hunt clipboard.

"It's looking good for Team Clemaron!" shouted my partner.

Then Amanda started taking the orange circus peanuts they'd bought out of the bag. As she chewed each one slowly and deliberately with her rosebud mouth, I tried to do the math in my head.

"Wait a minute," I said after she'd already swallowed almost the entire bag (math takes me a while), "even if you eat all of those you're still a point under us."

"Ha!" said Renee. "Not with these."

She opened up Amanda's tote and pulled out a pair of boxers. They had little snowmen on them. I wondered briefly if they were decoys, or if all Ethan's underwear was patterned in this cutesy way, or if he had some serious briefs tucked in his drawer somewhere and these were just the for-show versions we were seeing.

"You went over there too," Aaron said.

"Did Grandpa Garrison sing to you?" I asked.

"I didn't go over there said Amanda. "I just had these at my house."

I looked at her with a question in my eyes, and she smiled back at me. Then, when everyone else looked away she mouthed, "I'll tell you later." I could see her eyes shining with excitement as she popped the last orange circus peanut in her mouth, winning the scavenger hunt. And I felt a pang in my chest. Ethan had been at her house. He left his boxers there. Maybe they had been naked together.

And she hadn't told me.

chapter twelve

I wake up to a soft knock at my door. When Olive peeks in, she's wearing a headband with a purple bow on top of her short hair.

"What's the occasion?" I ask, rubbing my eyes. I didn't mean to fall asleep, but now that I'm waking up, I'm glad I did. Naps are the best.

"We're going out to dinner," says Olive.

"We're wha—?" I start. But then I remember. Red James, his father. Dinner on their boat.

I cover my head with a pillow.

"Where's James's mom, anyway?" asks Olive. "It's just him and his dad on the boat, right?"

"Do I look like James's biographer?"

Olive frowns like she's thinking hard.

"And don't bring it up tonight, Livy," I continue. "That's not something you can ask about. Maybe they're divorced or something. We have no idea."

"I am not a social moron," says Olive in a matter-of-fact way that makes her sound twenty years older than she is.

Then she becomes ten again. "I think James likes you," she singsongs.

I sit up and face her. "Just because he was talking to me doesn't mean he likes me," I say. "He's the kind of guy who talks to everyone. He's maniacally happy."

I think about his big smile then. It's true—he's always so upbeat.

"What are you smiling at?" asks Olive.

I straighten my mouth. "Nothing. Now get out of here so I can get dressed."

"Wear something pretty!" says Olive as she shuts the door behind her.

Hmph.

I look at the clock and realize we're supposed to be over there in ten minutes. No time for even a navy shower. I take off my clean-the-boat sweatshirt and jeans and put on a short-sleeved cotton sweater and slightly better dark-wash jeans. It's not like I have actual *nice* clothes on the boat with me. I don't even have any accessories; how did Olive think to pack things like headbands? I run a brush through my hair and twist it up into a loose bun, hoping that will do. I even swipe on some lip gloss—my first makeup in weeks. Then I pinch my cheeks for color and smile. I'm surprised at how easily my mouth turns up; I've been having to work at smiling lately. But tonight it feels almost natural.

Our family of four steps out onto the dock in the fading sunlight. Dad's in khakis and Top-Siders. Mom's wearing a white V-neck T-shirt and blue linen pants, Olive's got her bow, and I'm in lip gloss. We must look like the cover of *Boating Life* magazine.

Earlier, I was dreading tonight, but now I feel kind of . . . I don't know, hopeful? I'm determined to be normal. To stop thinking about Ethan. To see if I can get some of my old self back.

"Welcome aboard!" says Bill when we arrive at their slip. I notice that he's changed into a button-down and practically the same khakis as my dad, and I'm glad I fixed myself up a little. Then James ducks out from under the mainsail. He's got on a royal blue polo shirt that makes his eyes look like the ocean.

"Hey," he says, holding out a hand to help me step aboard. I take it, but not because I need it.

"That shirt really makes your hair stand out," I say. I don't know why I said that. I think I want to avoid telling him his eyes are, like, the most beautiful eyes I've ever seen.

"Uh, thanks." He runs a hand over his head. "Oh, I got us something."

He goes down below and comes up again a few seconds later carrying three root beers with straws. They're those old-fashioned glass-bottled root beers.

Olive claps her hands together. "Those are Clem's favorite thing!" she says.

James leans over so Olive can take her drink, then he hands one to me.

"Cheers," he says, and the three of us clink root beers.

I stare down at the thick glass lip as I finger the striped bendy straw (also a favorite). I can see the sunset colors in the glass—pink, orange, yellow—and for a moment, I feel fizzy and content, with nothing else on my mind.

I take a long sip and look over at my parents. They're lifting mugs of foamy beer in a toast while they smile at James's dad. Maybe this'll be a good night.

At dinner, Bill tells stories about his at-sea adventures, and he and Dad laugh loudly together as they try to outdo each other with nautical talk. I mostly have no idea what they're saying, but it doesn't matter, because their energy is contagious. Mom intervenes to correct Dad on details sometimes, but Bill just tells her that he would never want the truth to get in the way of a good boating story.

That makes Olive giggle.

The inside of the Townsends' boat is warm and cozy—all dark wood with lots of brass accents. I notice a red net hanging from the galley ceiling that's full of bananas—James wasn't kidding. None of them are browning, though. They must be today's supply. And I don't smell a hint of old-banana in here, which is incredible if you think about it.

There's a shelf full of navigation books above the portholes, and next to the ladder stairs up to the cockpit, I see a family portrait like the ones you get taken in a department-store photo studio. There are definitely three people in it, and the kid in the picture, who looks about five or six, has flaming red hair. I can't make out much more from my seat on the other side of the cabin, but I resolve to get a closer peek at it later.

I have another root beer when James offers, and I practically inhale the spaghetti marinara that Bill made. Olive does too. I think we're a little tired of Mom's canned wonder-meals, and the marinara is totally delicious—thick and oniony. I can see crushed tomato bits in the sink, so I know Bill from-scratched the sauce.

"I made the garlic bread!" says James when Bill gets compliments from all of us on the meal.

"You *buttered* the garlic bread," says his dad, knocking his elbow with affection.

The two of them are so at ease together, such a team. I look over at Olive watching them, and I know she's still wondering about James's mom, just like I am.

I have to pee, but I hate using other people's heads. You can hear the pee hitting the sides of the toilet—always—and half the time the flusher is too weak and toilet paper bubbles back up. Don't even get me started on the issues of having to go number two. So I hold it.

When James collects the dishes at the end of the meal, there's not a single noodle left on my plate.

"I had no idea I was so hungry," I say. "I'm stuffed!"

James laughs. "Don't worry. We can stretch out and do a dock walk while Dad keeps your parents captive here with more authentic tales from the sea."

"Hey," says Bill, "the Williamses are holding their own in the sailing stories department."

"Did I ever tell you about the time my father took us up to the Cape and we ran into some Kennedy cousins in a rowboat?" asks Mom.

I can feel Olive roll her eyes. This one we've heard over a hundred times.

"Is that our exit cue?" asks James.

"Yes!" huffs Olive.

The three of us finish clearing the table. Bill doesn't get up, and I wonder if James does this every night, if one of his jobs as first mate is to clean. I'm guessing yes. I'll have to mention that to Olive.

"Going for a walk," says James as we head above deck. He grabs a tote bag from the cockpit and slings it over his arm.

Bill nods and my parents don't even look our way—they're caught up in the stories of the night.

Outside it's dark and the air is mercifully cooler than earlier in the day—it feels like it's in the low seventies. We gently step off the boat and start to walk down the dock.

"Man, my dad can just talk and talk," says James.

"Maybe you should be thankful for his banana habit," I say. "It probably keeps his mouth occupied sometimes."

I hope that didn't sound rude or weird, but when I glance up at James I see that he's smiling. I like people who aren't too sensitive.

Then a tortoiseshell cat darts out in front of us.

"Mrs. Ficklewhiskers!" I shout.

"Mrs. *what*now?" asks Olive.

"She belongs to Ruth and George," I say. "I met them in Peoria on the dock. They're—"

"They're trouble," says James, jumping in.

"Who's trouble?" asks a raspy voice from behind us. I see Ruth coming up the dock with an open can of tuna in her hand.

"You are, little lady," says James, pointing at her. And I realize he must know them already.

Ruth giggles and takes James's arm. She looks at Olive and hands her the tuna.

"Here, take this to Mrs. Ficklewhiskers over there, will you?" she asks.

Olive runs over to the end of the dock and puts the can down for the cat, who sniffs it haughtily and then starts to take tiny bites.

I turn back to Ruth.

"Jimmy and I have been on this same route every summer since . . ." She stops. "Well, for four years or so, anyway. Right, Jimmy?"

"That's right," James says, giving her arm a squeeze.

It's sweet when guys are nice to older people. I take out my phone and snap a photo of them.

"Hey, I wasn't ready, was I?" says Ruth.

"I'm into candids," I say.

"She *loooves* candids," says my sister, running back from cat duty. She stares up at Ruth. "I'm Olive."

"Olive and Clementine and Jimmy, enjoying a night stroll," says Ruth, taking a deep breath. "Isn't that lovely?"

I hear George coming up the dock, and then he shouts, "Good for you, boy! That Clementine's a pretty one!"

"Oh, George, stop!" says Ruth. "The boy'll turn as red as his hair."

I hope they don't notice that my laugh sounds nervous and that I'm blushing too.

"Come on, my love," says George. "Our dreams await us."

He takes Ruth's hand and leads her away from James. They walk by Mrs. Ficklewhiskers and pick up the tuna can. She follows them back to their boat.

"You're good with older women, *Jimmy*," I say, teasing.

"Yeah, well, spend summers on a boat and you're pretty much rolling like the AARP set," he says. "Old people rule, but you guys are a very welcome surprise this year."

He grins at Olive, who beams back at him, and we continue our walk.

I fall silent, thinking about Ruth and George, how silly they seem, but also kind of wise or something. And how he called her "my love," which sounded so tender and sweet.

James and Olive banter back and forth about which boats are the nicest, and they argue about whether pontoon boats are a blast (Olive) or majorly cheesy (James). I listen to the chatter of their voices without really hearing their words. I'm still in my own world a little bit, finding it hard to stay in present moments.

But then James puts his hand on my shoulder.

"I have an idea," he says. "Let's go there." He points off toward the end of Pier 3, where neither of our boats are docked.

"We just walked Pier 3," says Olive. "Don't you remember? You said you love that giant yacht at the end, and I said my dad would say that's not a real boater's vessel, that's a ship for fools!"

I laugh. I didn't hear Olive say that the first time, but that totally is what Dad would say. It's a motorboat that must be almost sixty feet long. It's got tinted windows and a double-level cockpit with a spiral staircase leading up to a flybridge that's the perfect suntanning deck. I can't even imagine what's inside, but there are probably, like, five bedrooms.

"You want to see that boat *again*?" asks Olive.

"I want to go *on* that boat," says James. "I've been watching it all day—the owner is definitely not around. They probably left it for the week and just use it on the weekends."

He's looking at me with those blue eyes that match his blue shirt. His face is just a few inches from mine. And suddenly I don't have a problem being in the present moment.

"I don't know . . . ," says Olive.

"Stop being a baby," I say, holding James's stare. It's not like I'm a badass or like I've ever gone onto someone else's boat before, but why not? "Let's go."

We climb onto the side deck easily. There's gorgeous teak that my dad would definitely appreciate if he let himself get close enough to this boat, but he wouldn't, because it's not a sailboat and Dad doesn't do motorboats.

"Let's go up to the flybridge," says James. We climb the spiral stairs to the top level and I sit down, putting my legs up on one of the long seats, while Olive perches nervously at the helm next to the captain's wheel. James sits across from me and stretches out on the other seat. We're looking up at the dark sky, but it's a cloudy night and I can only see a handful of stars.

"I have never wanted to be an astronaut," says James.

I laugh.

"The sky is completely overwhelming," I say.

"Exactly," he says. "I mean, who in their right mind would want to *leave our planet*? For what? A closer look at the moon?"

"No thanks," I say.

"I think it'd be fun," says Olive.

"You're crazy, Olive," says James. "Would you hate it if I called you that all summer, 'Crazy Olive'?"

Did he say *all summer*?

I hear my little sister giggle. I sit up and look over at her; she's relaxing a little, leaning back in the captain's chair and staring up with us. I settle back down.

"I like being Crazy Olive," says my sister. "Better than being Boring Olive."

"Good point," says James. "Boring is the *worst*. It's better to be almost anything than bored."

"Even depressed, like Clem?" Olive says.

My head snaps up. I know she was joking, going on with the crazy thing, but that's not funny.

"Shut it, Olive," I say sharply.

She looks over at me with wide eyes, realizing she hit a nerve that she didn't mean to touch.

"What in the world could Clem have to be depressed about?" asks James, still staring at the sky, still using a light and teasing tone. "She's out here on a beautiful summer night, aboard this luxury vessel with Crazy Olive and Handsome James, whose blue shirt makes his red hair stand out."

I smile in spite of myself. He's paying attention to every word I say.

"And besides, I want you guys smiling for this next part," he continues.

"Next part?" I ask.

He sits up and whips a sketchbook and a dark gray pencil out of the tote he's been carrying.

He glances over at Olive, who looks enchanted, and then at me.

"Perfect," he says. And he starts to draw.

While he's drawing, he asks us to stay quiet so he can capture our "still selves." But he keeps talking, making us laugh. "Have you guys ever noticed that when you need ChapStick it's like you'd pay any amount of money to have it *right now*? Like your lips are about to flake off your face and you need the sweet relief that only that tube of petroleum-based product can bring?"

Listening to him is like being at the dentist in the chair with your mouth open and full of tools while the dentist asks you how school's going. I try to indicate with my eyes that I know what he means about the ChapStick, because I do, but I'm not sure I'm good at ocular communication—especially in the almost dark.

James keeps talking. "But then when you don't need Chap-Stick and everything is fine with your lips' moisture level, you'll find like twenty half-used tubes at the bottom of your backpack from the times when you were completely desperate for the stuff."

He shakes his head.

"So weird. This is what I think about while I draw."

His hands keep moving the whole time, faster than his mouth even, and I wonder how anything that moves so fast could be creating a drawing that's even remotely good. But after about twenty minutes, James gets up suddenly and holds the sketch pad right in front of our faces, and what I see surprises me.

Olive gasps.

"That's so us!" she says, delighted.

It's a cartoon us—not like one of those real-life portrait drawings, but still, she's right. James got her face perfectly: the way her nose turns up a little at the end, her slightly mussy left eyebrow, the glint of light that bounces off her green-framed glasses, which are a tiny bit askew in real life and in the drawing.

I notice that the background isn't this setting, aboard this huge yacht. It's earlier, at sunset. You can tell even in his gray pencil that the "lighting" is from a few hours ago. Olive and I are sipping from our root beer bottles. James put himself in the scene, too, just a little. His glass bottle is reaching in to touch ours for a "cheers."

And then I look at me. I mean, illustrated me. She's prettier than I am. She has freckles on her nose and a smile playing on her lips, though she's not letting it spread across her face. Her hair is pulled back in a bun, like mine, and the arch of her cheekbones is striking—like she has a face that's meant to be drawn. Her eyes look bright and alive, but there's no doubt they look sad too.

I glance up at James and see him studying me. I wonder how much he can read in my face.

"We should go," I say.

"Don't you like it, Clem?" asks Olive.

I bite my lip and look down at her. "It's great," I say, though I feel like I might start to cry.

I walk to the spiral stairs and carefully but quickly ease myself down to the main deck. Then I step off the side of the boat and onto the dock. As the wake of a passing motorboat makes its way into the marina and rocks the dock with a few waves, I suddenly remember that I have to pee. *Badly.*

"You guys, I'm going to *The Possibility*," I shout. "James, can you take Olive back to your boat?"

"Clem, wait!" says James. He's down the steps in a flash. "Is there something wrong?"

"No!" I say. "I just really have to pee."

And it's only a half lie, because I *do* have to pee, and I have to pee *right now*. I'm almost glad for this slightly comical distraction, because I don't want James to know that what's actually wrong is that he saw it. He saw my sadness.

I hustle toward *The Possibility* and look back once to be sure

Olive is with James and they're walking to his boat. Then I run-walk back to our boat, jump on board, and tear down the stairs into the head.

Ahhhh. Does anything feel better than making it to a bathroom after you've been holding it for hours? Well, probably something, but I can't think of what in this instance. Sweet relief.

I sit in the main cabin of the boat for a minute. I could do the right thing and walk back over to *Dreaming of Sylvia*, say good night to James and his dad properly, thank them for a nice night.

But I just stay on the couch and listen to the gentle waves lap against the side of *The Possibility*. Those eyes. *My* eyes. They were cartoons, but they were so real. I saw my own sadness in that drawing, like I was looking into a reflecting pool from a fantasy novel that showed me my soul or something. How could James see that?

chapter thirteen

Dear Amanda,
It's so hard to hide things from you. I know
you sensed something was wrong...

⛵

"I saw your feelings get hurt," said Amanda. We'd just gotten home from the movies with Ethan and Renee and Henry, and she was sitting on my bed, staring into the mirror across the room.

"What?" I asked.

"Just that I could see it in your face when me and Ethan were holding hands," she said.

"Oh." My heart pounded in my chest.

Amanda's mom is a therapist, and everyone in her family is way tuned in to their own emotions, and others' feelings too—it's actually kind of annoying how hard it is to hide anything from my best friend.

Amanda took a deep breath.

"What?" I asked.

I watched her squeeze her eyes shut in the mirror.

"I know it's kind of awkward," she said. Then she opened them. "But I think it's normal that you're jealous that I have a boyfriend who's actually hanging out with us now."

"Oh, I'm not," I said, surprised. "I like Ethan . . ." I was about to add "a lot," but I decided to leave it at that.

"Okay, okay." She smiled at me, relieved. "I just had to say something, because it seems like you guys are friends, and then he and I are going out, so it's like you have these two friends dating and it can be weird because we spend time alone, too, and . . . I don't know, am I rambling?"

"No." I kept my participation in this conversation very measured.

"It's cool that you guys get along," she said, and I saw her eyes widen a little in the mirror. "You seem to always be talking or having, like, private jokes."

I wondered if she was fishing for something, if she could read me that well.

"We have a class together," I said.

"I know," she said, and then she threw her arms around me. "I'm sorry, Clem, I didn't mean to say that you were jealous! It just seemed like something was bothering you tonight, is all."

I nodded and hugged her back. "It's nothing," I said. "Maybe I am a little jealous because he takes away my time with you."

That was an acceptable thing to be jealous about, so I went with it.

"Let's have a sleepover next weekend," said Amanda. "Just you and me."

"Sounds good." I pulled away from our hug and smiled brightly at her.

"Ack, sorry I made things awkward!" she said. Then she waved her hands in front of my face, which I guess looked kind of grim. "Okay, forget all that. Want me to make you a smile?"

And that was that. Amanda had noticed something wrong, and I had my warning—and I didn't heed it. I had proof then that the weirdness wasn't just in my head. I knew for sure that I needed to stop talking to Ethan so much.

But I didn't. It was like I couldn't help it.

Later that week, one snowy afternoon when I was stuck in the house, Ethan and I spent over three hours online, messaging different song lyrics to each other and trying to guess the song.

> **Clem:** I am so homesick for someplace I will never be
> **Ethan:** The Bravery, Time Won't Let Me Go
> **Ethan:** When the wind is in your hair you laugh like a little girl
> **Clem:** Easy. Magnetic Fields, Luckiest Guy on the Lower East Side
> **Ethan:** How very indie-aware of you

I laughed.

> **Clem:** I was dreaming of the past . . . and my heart was beating fast

He replied in, like, 0.4 seconds.

> **Ethan:** Jealous Guy, John Lennon
> **Clem:** You are so freaking good at this

Clem: That's an obscure song!

Ethan: Nothing John Lennon ever did is obscure

And this is something I liked about him too. We had this shared musical sensibility. Whenever he mentioned a song that I didn't know, I instantly had to download it and listen, and I always ended up loving it. That's just how we aligned. It felt special. Plus, he never once made an "Oh my darlin' . . ." joke about my name, which was pretty much a first. You don't have a name like Clementine without having that song sung at you at least three times a week.

Clem: I'm still impressed

Ethan: She's so scared, so very frightened

Clem: Vague . . . more?

Ethan: Anything could happen . . . right here tonight

Ethan: That's all you get (not a lyric)

Clem: Old song?

Ethan: Yup

Clem: Like oldie old or 90s old?

Ethan: More like 80s

Clem: Band?

Ethan: Cheating, but ok—INXS

Clem: No clue, don't really know them.

Ethan: It's called Beautiful Girl

My hands froze.

Ethan: I'll put it on your mix

That's when he told me he was making me a playlist of songs that reminded him of me. And the one I knew about was called—good Lord—"Beautiful Girl." I downloaded it and fell in love within the first six notes.

All I could think about was how much I wanted that playlist. I had never felt so excited and tingly and buzzy about a guy.

I copied and pasted our back-and-forth messaging session into a doc, then put it in a folder that, for stealth's sake, I called "Every Once in a While." That's the name of a country song that my mom always turned up the volume for in the car, and it makes me feel warm inside to hear it.

That's when I started planning a mix for him too. The first song on it? "You Belong With Me" by Taylor Swift. I was in deep.

chapter fourteen

We're heading into the Mississippi River now, and Olive keeps mentioning *The Adventures of Huckleberry Finn.*

"Did you read that last summer in your advanced library program for kids with glasses?" I ask.

She sticks out her tongue at me.

I'm trying to read an outdated issue of *Us Weekly* that I picked up at the last dock deli, but once Olive starts in with the Huck Finn talk, she won't leave me alone until I respond. "Do you think Huck and Jim were on this part of the river? Is this what they saw from the raft? Don't you think it seems a lot bigger than it did in the book?" She gets on my nerves so much that finally, as we're sitting above deck eating peanut butter and jelly sandwiches together and trying to direct Dad around the floating orange buoys that mark the dangerous parts of the river, I snap, "I get it! You're smart. You've read Mark Twain and you're only ten. Everyone on this boat *knows!*"

Olive frowns. "I was just trying to have a discussion about a book we've both read," she says. "*Excuuuuuse* me!"

It's silent for a minute, and I take a bite of my sandwich.

"Olive," I say when I finish swallowing. "I'm sorry I shouted."

"That's okay." She's already recovered and smiling again. "I know you're just mad that I'm smarter than you are."

I give her a patronizing grin.

"Clem?" she asks.

"Livy?"

"Do you think James looks like Huck Finn?"

I laugh. "You never give up!"

"Well, do you?" she asks. "Do you think he's like Huck at all?"

"Um, I guess I don't really know. Did Huck have red hair?"

"Not really," says Olive. "But I think he has Huck's pluck."

"Huck's pluck?" I ask. "Where did you get that?"

"My teacher, Mrs. Perry, told me I had Huck's pluck," she says. "I like the way it sounds. Besides, I do think he has pluck. Look!"

I glance over to where Olive's pointing behind me, and I see that *Dreaming of Sylvia* is just a few hundred feet in the distance.

"Wow," I say, crossing my arms over my chest. *They really are following our same route.*

"I'll get the binoculars," says Olive. Before I can stop her, she's going down through the hatch and into Dad's nav station. She's back in a minute and hands me a big black case.

"You spy on him," I say. "You're the one who cares so much about what he's doing."

"You don't like him, Clem?" asks Olive. "I think he's really fun."

She smiles, and I swear I almost see a hint of a blush. I'm about to tease her, but then I remember how awful that can be when you're first starting to like boys. So I refrain.

The binoculars cover almost all of Olive's face, and she leans on her elbows to help her balance as we hit some waves. I snap a phone pic of her because she looks so silly. A bit of spray comes up onto the boat and she has to pause to wipe off the glass lenses, but finally she gets a good long look.

Then she giggles.

"What?" I ask.

"Nothing," she says. "I thought you weren't interested."

"I'm not. But if you're going to have, like, *reactions* to what's going on, of course I'm curious."

Olive smiles at me like she knows something. I turn halfheartedly back to my magazine.

"He's whistling," she says after a minute.

"You can't hear that from here," I say.

"I can tell. His lips are pursed and he's snapping his fingers every once in a while."

"Let me see that," I say. And then I add, "It sounds ridiculous," so Olive doesn't think I'm interested in watching James.

She's right. He *is* whistling. And he gets this huge grin on his face in between whistling sessions. Has this guy ever known a dark day?

I hand the binoculars back to Olive.

"It appears that you're right," I say. "He is whistling."

"He could make you happy," says Olive.

"What?" I ask. "What are you talking about?"

"I just mean that you're sad and he's not, and when he's around— even through binoculars—you smile more," says my sister.

"I do not."

"You do too," she says. "It's almost like the old you."

"Well, who wouldn't laugh at a guy who's whistling to himself like a freak?" I sound meaner than I want to. I pick up my magazine. "Put the binoculars back in the nav station before Dad sees they're gone," I say to Olive.

She pauses and stares at me for a minute before disappearing dutifully down the hatch.

I look back at *Dreaming of Sylvia* and see James, a tiny little stick figure dancing around on the deck. I used to be happy like that. Didn't I?

chapter fifteen

Dear Amanda,
I didn't realize that, sometimes, even if a
situation is getting out of control, it happens
slowly, in these really small moments. And even
if what's happening is wrong, it can feel like
it's right.
*   I got so wrapped up in the fact that*
something was happening. Someone was into
me. I didn't have to be boring old Clem all
the time. I had a secret.

I crumple up the paper and add it to the wad of trashed Letters to Amanda in my bottom drawer.

"Don't you guys think that show about those people in the sixties who drink all the time and treat women like crap is weird?" said

Amanda at lunch one day. "I mean, it's kind of glorifying that behavior, in a way."

And I guess she had a point or whatever, but it was more like a class topic than something fun to discuss at lunch when your brain is allowed to be off for a minute.

Ethan nodded halfheartedly and kissed her cheek.

I said, "Yeah, true."

I was eating a leftover slice of pizza with mushrooms on it. "Mushrooms are so emotionally satisfying," I said.

Ethan's face lit up. "YES! I've always thought that. It's something about their consistency and how they're both soft and a little rubbery but also meaty in a way, right?"

I smiled. That was *exactly* what I meant. "Like how a portobello can sub in for a burger. I mean, seriously, that is a major move by a vegetable."

"I know!" Ethan said. "It's like, 'Oh, today I'll just top your salad, but maybe tomorrow I'll stick myself between a bun and be your main meal.'"

"Very versatile." I nod. "And international! I mean, give me some Japanese shiitakes in broth, please."

"Medicinal, too," said Ethan, leaning forward over the table. "Did you know that mushrooms are anti-inflammatory and have antiviral properties?"

"I did not know that, but I'm not surprised," I said. "They're kind of food superheroes."

Then I glanced at the rest of the table and saw that they were staring at us in silence. For a moment it had been just me and Ethan and mushroom talk.

"Fungi nerds," said Henry, turning back to his sandwich.

Amanda smiled at us happily. The guys she'd dated before

didn't really fit in with our friends. They were nice and every-thing, but just not guys I'd talk to for long periods of time. Ethan seemed different already.

When the bell rang, Ethan asked Amanda if she was free on Friday to go to *Red Water,* this indie film festival–winning movie that I'd been dying to see.

I laughed a little bit, anticipating her response.

"Or maybe the new Kate Hudson?" she said. "It's playing right downtown."

"Sure," said Ethan, and I gave him a sympathetic glance.

Amanda saw. "You know, I'm not into the emo-indie stuff—you should go with Clem."

I froze mid–Dr Pepper can toss.

"I wouldn't want to get in the way of your shared super-geekdom," said Amanda. "Maybe there'll even be a scene with mushrooms in it!"

I studied her face for a moment, but all I could see was a sunny smile and total ease.

"You up for it, Clem?" asked Ethan. "I hate going to movies alone."

⛵

He picked me up in his mom's Pontiac—I needed a ride, I'd told Ethan, and he didn't hesitate to offer.

I got in and we smiled, and it was like, *should we hug or some-thing?,* but we didn't, we just sat there, and then he said, "Awk-ward," and I laughed, and he started to drive and it felt okay again.

"Have you ever played the song game?" I asked him. We were heading out of my neighborhood, winding down the back road to the highway.

"The song game?"

"I'll take that as a no," I said. "The song game is when you pick a radio station or shuffle your music, and then you tell the universe that the next song that comes on is how someone else feels about you."

"Huh?" he asked.

"I'm bad at explaining." We were listening to this classic rock station and "Under My Thumb" by the Rolling Stones was playing.

I tried to clarify. "Okay, so for example, the next song that comes on the radio will express how you feel about me."

"Whoa," he said. "This game is intense."

He smiled and rubbed his hands on the steering wheel. "Make it a good one, DJ!"

I laughed as the DJ came on to announce the next track.

When "I Want You to Want Me" by Cheap Trick came on, I got goose bumps and stared straight ahead at the road.

Even Ethan seemed lost for a way to lighten the moment as the lyrics went on and on . . . "I'd love you to love me."

"Wow, that game really works," he said after a minute. He said it quietly, and I could tell he wasn't entirely joking.

I looked over at him and smiled, knowing then that we were getting close to crossing a line. I'd played the song game with all of my friends before. But if I got that song for, like, Aaron or Henry, they probably would have made some crude joke about wanting to get in my pants, and we would have laughed about it. It wouldn't have meant anything. This felt different.

Because the movie we were seeing was an artsy one, we had to drive half an hour out of town to this classic old theater that only shows those kinds of movies. You know, the ones that get nominated for awards but that don't really play at the stadium-seating, crazy-big screen places.

"I love this theater," I said as I got out of the car.

"It's amazing," said Ethan. "Look at the marquee!"

"I know." The title of the movie was up in these huge three-foot-high letters, and the stars' names were listed underneath, like you'd see in some old Hollywood scene. "That's my favorite thing about this place. Well, aside from the real butter they serve on the popcorn."

"No way," said Ethan, his eyes lighting up.

"Totally," I said. "We can share a large."

"Awesome." And then, just like that, he took my hand in his. He held it for a beat before he dropped it and looked at me. His expression seemed wistful.

"Sorry," he said.

"It's okay." I went straight up to the ticket box so he couldn't see my face getting red.

We did share popcorn, but we got separate sodas. He wanted Sprite, but I'm strictly a Dr Pepper girl. We didn't talk about the fact that he had essentially held my hand, but I could tell it was hanging there in the air, filling the spaces between our shared laughter at the movie—which was excellent—and the times when our fingers would brush against each other in the popcorn bag.

On the ride home, we changed the radio to one of those "eighties, nineties, and today" stations, and we played the song game two more times. Once for how Amanda felt about Ethan (we got "Romeo and Juliet" by Taylor Swift, which made me squirm, it was so sickly lovey) and once for how my camp boyfriend Steve felt about me (we got "Beat It" by Michael Jackson, which made us both laugh).

"I guess he's over you," said Ethan. "Hard as that is to imagine."

I know I should have been mad at him for saying things like

that, for making the air between us full of that delicious kind of awkward all the time.

But I loved the way Ethan made me feel.

⛵

"Do we think ranch dressing drizzled over popcorn is tasty or gross?"

"Tasty." I held out the bowl so Amanda could administer creamy white goodness.

She paused. "It might make it soggy."

"Drizzle," I said.

Very carefully, she moved the bottle over the popcorn bowl.

Olive wandered into the kitchen. "Sick!"

"What did I tell you?" I asked Olive.

Her eyes went wide. "To be quiet if I wanted to hang out with you guys."

"Right."

She frowned and I ruffled her hair. I was actually glad to have her around that night.

"Want me to pop you a separate batch, Livy?" asked Amanda.

"Yes, please," said my sister.

Amanda grabbed another microwavable sack out of the cabinet.

"Not everyone has our exotic tastes, Clem," she said, smiling over her shoulder as she pressed the "Popcorn" setting.

I grinned and took a handful of ranch-covered popcorn.

"Verdict?" asked Amanda.

I held up my messy fingers. "We should probably invest in flavored salt," I said. "It's drier."

Amanda laughed and handed me a paper towel.

The night after I went to the movies with Ethan, Amanda and

I were preparing to watch an old favorite, *The Little Mermaid,* in the den. Olive pulled a beanbag chair out from her room and settled onto the floor.

Usually I'm not that into having my little sister around for sleepovers, but I was afraid of being alone with Amanda that night.

Besides, it was sort of a throwback evening for us. We hadn't had a *sleepover* sleepover, like with popcorn and Disney movies and BFF secrets, since sixth grade. The thing was, I didn't really want to do the BFF-secrets part. Because now I had my own secret, one that I had to admit to myself: I liked Ethan.

But that night was about me and Amanda. I thought it might stop the weird swirl of thoughts I was having about Ethan.

When Ariel's best song came on, Amanda stood up and held the remote in front of her like a microphone.

"Look at this stuff . . . isn't it neat?" she sang along. "Wouldn't you think my collection's complete?"

I stood and chimed in. Olive looked at us like we were nuts, but Amanda and I finished out the whole song, belting into our awful high ranges (meaning just raising the volume) for the final lines.

Then we collapsed onto the couch giggling.

"I think we should audition for a singing show," said Amanda, trying to straighten her grin.

I shook my head, stifling a laugh. "It really wouldn't be fair to the other contestants."

Olive rolled her eyes and we settled down again, sipping our sodas through bendy straws and eating our ever-more-soggy popcorn. Everything felt right.

By the time Ariel was on land with Prince Eric, Olive was asleep. I let her doze, and when the credits rolled, I woke her up and walked her sleepy self to bed.

"I'll get this," said Amanda, gathering a tray with the popcorn bowl and our glasses. She must have put them in the kitchen and then gone to my room, because when I got there after tucking in Olive, Amanda was staring at the bulletin board over my desk.

"What's this for?" she asked.

She was fingering the list of songs I had planned for Ethan's playlist. It was pinned up to the board because I'd been brainstorming in history class and I wanted to remember to download the music to my desktop. *How could I have just left it up there?*

Did her voice sound suspicious? No. I was being paranoid. It was just a song list, not anything she could read into.

"'Girl from the North Country,' 'Skinny Love,' 'Last Goodbye'!" She laughed loudly, her eyes wide. "These are your *favorites*. You're totally in love with someone! Who is it?"

I started to sweat. I could actually feel wetness pooling in my armpits. Gross, but true.

"It's just a playlist I was thinking about," I said. "For, um, STEVE!"

I shouted the name of my camp boyfriend loudly, and it sounded weird, probably because I'd just thought of it as it came out of my mouth.

"Steve?" asked Amanda, tilting her head to the left. "Sailing-camp Steve?"

"Yeah," I said.

"You haven't talked about him since two summers ago," she said.

"He messaged me the other day, so we've been back in touch." I walked over to the bulletin board and took down the song list. "He's gotten hotter," I said, adding a detail that I thought made my story sound more authentic.

Note to self: look up Steve again and make him a playlist. It's not a lie if you make it true after the fact, right?

Amanda sat down on my bed and stretched out her legs, leaning back against the wall. "Wasn't he the one who was really into metal?" she asked. "Didn't you say that was part of the reason you guys couldn't last through fall?"

She was smiling and amused, but I felt myself being pulled deeper and deeper into deception-land.

"Yeah, I'm hoping to expand his musical tastes and give it another shot," I said. My story didn't sound remotely believable.

"Doesn't he live in, like, Kentucky?"

How was her memory so good?

"It could work," I said, joining her on the bed and looking into the mirror across the wall.

Her reflection eyed mine in the glass. "Clem, you're so busted."

"Huh?"

"Just tell me who you like!" she said. "Really."

Her smile was open and wide, ready to listen to a good crush story, ready to go over tiny little details—like what this amazing guy said to me in the hallways or how he looked at me across a classroom.

"Noah Knight," I said, naming the first hot-but-not-in-our-universe guy who came to mind. He was a skater, and I'd probably exchanged two words with him during our entire school career, but he seemed plausible because he'd suddenly gotten drop-dead over the summer.

Amanda put her hand to her heart. "He's a total dream," she said, her eyes shining. "Okay, I'm in. Let me know what I can do to help."

I smiled at her in the mirror, and there in the reflection it looked like a real BFF smile. But I was glad she wasn't looking at my actual face.

chapter sixteen

Dear Amanda,
I didn't mean to lie to you. I tried to stop
it, you know. I talked to Ethan one day
after school, and...

⛵

"Are you working at Razzy's today?" asked Ethan as we walked out of history together.

"Yeah, four to eight," I said. "Are you going to the mall?"

"Now that I know you're working I am," he said.

I felt a tightness in my chest—like excitement and guilt combined. More and more, our interactions felt like flirting. Not the harmless variety, but the actual prelude-to-a-relationship kind.

"I'll look for you," I said.

"I'll be there." He gave me a small wave as he turned left down the math hallway to meet Amanda by her locker.

What exactly was my problem?

Sometimes I thought I had this weird crush on Ethan because

I had only had that one boyfriend—Steve from sailing camp. Although it was a really sweet summer romance—and we even got to sneakily spend the night together in the craft cabin—it didn't really count in terms of school. Because camp boyfriends? They sound made up.

Until this year, I couldn't find anyone to date at Bishop Heights High. It was like no guys really *got* me. But Ethan did.

Why did it have to be Ethan?

⛵

At work that afternoon, I busied myself by restocking the candy—pouring peppermints and gumdrops into big glass jars and sticking long-stemmed lollipops into their display stands. But after twenty minutes, there was nothing to do but hang out in between customers. My weekday shifts were solo because it was never that busy, which was good for doing homework, and one reason why Mom and Dad let me keep this job during the school year.

I wasn't doing homework that day, though. I had torn up my list of songs for Ethan's playlist, and I brought my journal because I wrote down a promise to myself:

> If Ethan stops by tonight with Amanda, it's all good. We're friends, he knows that. If he shows up by himself, just to see me, I will tell him that I think we should stop hanging out. That it's not okay. That Amanda wouldn't like it.

There it was, in black and white. Somehow it felt like an official order to myself, since I wrote it down. But I couldn't figure out the wording I wanted to use if I did have to bring things up with Ethan, and I was still kind of unclear on what to say.

I was turning all of this over in my head, lost in my own world, when Ethan's smile hit me like a fastball.

"Hey," he said.

"Hi!" I stood up, greeting him too brightly, like he was a customer I wanted to impress. "Can I get you something?"

Now I was really acting like he was a customer.

"Aha," said Ethan. "So this can be an official candy-counter visit and not just a drop-by-to-see-Clem thing?"

He did come just to see me. Heart fluttered, heart sank.

"Is Amanda coming?" I asked, hoping, *really* hoping, she was.

"She tutors after school on Wednesdays," he said.

And I knew that, of course I knew that. I'd only been her friend for, like, a hundred years.

I glanced back down at the black ink in my journal to give me strength.

"So I made you something," said Ethan. "That's why I wanted to stop by, I mean."

"Oh," I said. "Uh, thanks."

"Wait to thank me—you haven't seen it yet." He reached into his coat pocket and brought out a CD. "I burned your playlist. I know it's kind of old school, but this way you have a hard copy, and I got to work on the cover and stuff."

I turned the plastic case over in my hand. In very messy, classic boy scrawl, I saw the names of some of the songs Ethan had chosen for me: "Beautiful Girl," "Zebra," "So Much Closer." Around the edges he'd doodled vines—ivy?—and the title said, "For Clementine, From Ethan." It wasn't exactly a declaration of love, but I still felt a stone in the pit of my stomach.

"I can't take this," I said, pushing it back across the counter toward him.

He looked surprised, maybe even hurt.

"Why not?"

"You know," I said. Not the most eloquent expression of what I wanted to say.

"What do I know?" asked Ethan.

I sighed in frustration.

"It's too much," I said. Again I was Queen Vague. I looked down at my journal, but it didn't have a script for me.

"Clem," said Ethan, leaning on the counter and spinning one of the rainbow lollipops with his fingers. "It really isn't a big deal. Amanda doesn't like the same music I do, and I love making mixes. I used to do it for all my friends back in Ohio."

"You did?"

"Yup." He let go of the lollipop and smiled at me. "Even the girls. My *friends*. My friends who were girls."

"Oh," I said again, still unsure.

"Guys and girls can be friends," said Ethan. "Like you and Aaron, right? Or you and Henry."

I looked down at the counter, my face reddening a little. *Was I just overreacting? Reading too much into this? Making myself look like a fool for thinking that Ethan was flirting with me when really he was just being my friend?*

"Cool," I said, finally, reaching out and taking the CD again. Part of me really wanted to hear the songs he chose. "Sorry for being . . . um . . ."

"It's okay," said Ethan.

And then he stayed. He stayed for another hour of my shift, stepping aside whenever a customer came and making me laugh in between.

"Serious question: Could a Sour Patch Kid take a Gummy Bear in a fight?"

I was getting zero homework done.

"Definitely," I said. "I've actually contemplated this matchup before. Sour Patch kids have sharp, scratchy skin, and they're kind of like the bad kids on the block—total bullies. Gummy Bears are just soft and sweet."

"But they're *bears*," said Ethan.

"Kid-sized bears, not big scary ones."

"I'm not convinced." Ethan turned his back to me and leaned on the counter.

I took out a red Sour Patch Kid and a green Gummy Bear to show Ethan how soft and gooey the Bears were compared to the Kids. He eventually relented.

And this is how our evening went. From serious to silly, from awkward to so comfortable.

When he left I had this big smile on my face. Things were okay. He'd made it clear that we were *friends*. That was all. Isn't that what I'd wanted to set straight? Mission accomplished.

I put the CD on the corner of my desk when I got home. I didn't need to hear it right away, I told myself.

Seven minutes later, I downloaded it to an iPod playlist.

I'd listened straight through twice by the time I fell asleep.

chapter seventeen

I've already finished the three books I was allowed to bring in hard-copy form, so I approach my mom about giving up her e-reader for the afternoon. I downloaded fifteen more titles there because, let's be real, I knew I'd have some downtime out on the water this summer. Getting Mom to let me take the e-reader out in the dinghy, on the other hand, is less of a sure thing.

"I'll keep it in this plastic bag and I'll be so, so careful," I promise her. "Please, I just need some . . . quiet time." I glance at my little sister, who's happily stripping a string cheese down to its last string while she hums a Lady Gaga song.

Mom looks at me sternly, but I can tell she's cracking.

"Do not splash, put it back in the bag if a big wake is coming, and under no circumstances are you to stand up or shift your weight while you're reading—just stay still and hold it far away from the water."

"No problem!" I nod enthusiastically and she hands it over. We're docked for the day, but even just floating in the dinghy while it's twenty feet from the boat is a relief. It feels like my own personal island.

I stretch out in the *Sea Ya* for an hour with a life jacket behind my head as a pillow and lose myself in a story about sisters, one of whom may or may not have magical powers. When I feel my eyelids getting heavy, I sink a little deeper into the life jacket and doze off.

Rocking waves wake me up, and I stretch and yawn—it feels like I've been out for just five minutes, but the sun has moved, so it was probably at least an hour. I should get back. I sit up and make sure the plastic bag is sealed around Mom's e-reader. Then I look around. I don't see *The Possibility*.

I realize that I've come untied from the boat (note to self: make Olive study Dad's copy of *The Complete Book of Knots* a little more closely). No big deal—I'm just across the inlet where the marina is, and I have a small engine.

I'm about to start it up when I hear a choked cry behind me. I turn around, and about twenty feet away, floating in his dinghy by an old fallen tree trunk, is Mr. Townsend. His shoulders are hunched, and he's looking down at the water. He has a fishing pole by his side, but he's not actively casting.

I'm about to call out to him, but then I see his back begin to shake, almost like he's . . . crying? I hear another big gulp from his direction, and it confirms that he's definitely in the middle of a weep session.

It's weird—he seems so big and strong, so boisterous and joyful. What is it that makes a guy like Mr. Townsend, a dad, go off to cry?

I bite my lip. Should I start up the engine now? He'll probably know I've seen him. I slink back down to my below-sightlines position in the boat and stay quiet. I stare at my thighs and see that the sun's been on them—they're getting warm and red. That reminds me of another night I wish I didn't remember. I don't want to let my thoughts spiral into a bad place; I have to get back to the boat.

Maybe I'm crazy, but I don't want to embarrass Mr. Townsend, so I recreate the whole scene again where I'm just waking up. From my invisible position, I make a big production of stretching and yawning superloudly, rocking the boat and banging up against the side before I raise my head and look around.

When I pop up again, he's looking my way with a big smile on his face. He's also holding his rod and getting ready to cast.

"Mr. Townsend!" I say, acting surprised.

"Hiya, Clem," he shouts. "Looks like you drifted a little bit far from home."

"I did," I say, marveling at how quickly he's turned from tears to this happy grin. "I guess Olive needs a little more knot practice."

He chuckles. "Send her over to James anytime—he's the expert."

"Will do," I say, saluting him. Something about being on the water makes you say things like "Will do" and make saluting gestures.

I crank up the engine and motor back to *The Possibility*, feeling good about helping Mr. Townsend avoid embarrassment. I know all about hiding things.

chapter eighteen

Dear Amanda,

~~Nothing ever really happened between me~~
~~and Ethan. It wasn't a big deal. We just~~
You always seemed so secure. Remember,
you even <u>told us</u> to go to the movies
together. It was almost easier for me to
justify because you acted so nonchalant...

After that day at Razzy's, I half convinced myself that Ethan and I were safely on the friendship track and not moving in any inappropriate directions. That way, I didn't have to feel guilty spending hours messaging him or listening to his mix. I know, it made no sense. He sometimes texted me when I knew he was out with Amanda. So even though we didn't have another "date" where it was just the two of us, we were still aboard the *Titanic*, heading for the iceberg. But it was worse than that—it was like we could see the looming disaster, or at least I could, but I still wouldn't turn the ship around.

"Corner!" I shouted as I ran downstairs to the big U-shaped couch in Amanda's basement.

She quickly slid into the other side. We always grabbed the corners because they're the best spots. We shared a smile as we got our seats, and then our other friends settled in around us. Ethan sat right between me and Amanda. They held hands. I looked straight ahead at the TV.

Henry chose the movie, so it was an old Spike Lee one—his film studies thing means he's got to see all the classics. I pretended to mind, but really I didn't, because a lot of them are classics for a reason, and *Do the Right Thing* is no exception.

But I had trouble concentrating.

"Pass the blanket?" I asked.

I'm always getting cold in other people's houses. Amanda even had a blue-and-white knit blanket on hand that I thought of as "my blanket" because I used it so much.

She let go of Ethan's hand, reaching over to the side chair where it hung, and tossed it to me.

"Thanks." I spread it over my legs. It's a big blanket so some fell across Ethan.

"Sorry," I said.

"It's okay, I get cold too."

Spike Lee was arriving at work at the pizza place, and suddenly I felt Ethan's hand resting on the side of my leg. It wasn't like that was insanely weird—I had jeans on!—but it was definitely not a friendly resting-my-hand-by-your-leg situation. It was a *romantic* resting-my-hand-by-your-leg situation.

Plus, there was the blanket, so it was also a no-one-else-can-see situation. I sat very still for the next half hour. So did he.

His light touch started to feel really comfortable, almost sooth-ing. I relaxed. This was okay. Maybe he didn't even know where his hand was. Maybe he thought he was touching a couch cushion.

But then his hand slid up to my thigh. Like, *on top of* my thigh.

I was so surprised, I wasn't sure what to do. I just stared straight ahead; I could see peripherally that he was doing that, too, pre-tending like nothing was happening, while I felt this tingling run through me as his hand started to caress my thigh, and it felt like *everything* was happening. But invisibly.

These really loud New York characters were talking. And Henry was laughing. And Amanda was offering people drinks and snacks. And Renee was getting up to go to the bathroom. And Aaron was talking about how Rosie Perez used to be hot. And all this time, Ethan was touching my thigh.

Everyone settled down again and focused on the movie, so I tried to move Ethan's hand away with my hand—I wasn't so delu-sional that I didn't know what we were doing was totally weird and wrong. But when I gently pushed his hand off my thigh, he held fast to mine, and we ended up holding hands under the blanket.

We sat that way for the rest of the movie, and every once in a while he would move his fingers a little and stroke my palm.

I know I should have snatched it away; I know his girlfriend—my best friend—was three feet to my left. She even turned to him to smile and laugh at the funny parts with the old guys on the street, and he looked right back at her, grinning. My mind was screaming, *We are holding hands!*

I gave up on trying to reach over and eat popcorn from the big bowl on the center of the coffee table, because then I would have had to let go of Ethan.

"Did I put too much salt on the popcorn, Clem?" asked Amanda.

"No, I'm just not hungry."

She gave me a weird look. Normally I can barrel through, like, three large bowls of popcorn by myself. It's one of those snacks magazines always tell you that you can eat a lot of and it's still kind of healthy, so I take full advantage.

But that night I hardly ate any at all. I barely moved.

I wrote a journal entry later when I got home:

> What am I doing? What is _he_ doing? It's not even like we were alone—everyone was <u>right there</u>. I know I'm a bad friend. I know I'm doing something terrible. I just don't know how to stop.

⛵

I'm sitting in my cabin, paging through my diary. Looking back at that entry, I can see that it's a cop-out. People know how to stop—they just _stop_. They stop holding their friends' boyfriends' hands under the blanket. It didn't _have_ to happen, even if Ethan wanted it to. I could have taken my hand and moved myself around in a way that he couldn't really get to me, and he would have had to stare straight ahead at the movie even if he was upset or angry, because he shouldn't have been doing what he was doing! He shouldn't have been trying to touch my leg and hold my hand!

What the eff was Ethan thinking? I may have gone along with everything, but he's the one who started it. He grabbed my hand at the movies, he made me a playlist, he rubbed my leg under his girlfriend's freaking blanket!

I slam my journal shut and lie back on my bed in a huff, staring at the ceiling. This isn't my fault, at least not completely. Does that even matter to Amanda? Does she even care about Ethan's part in this?

chapter nineteen

"Olive, seriously, stop." My voice has a hard edge, and my sister hears me this time. She's been sitting in the cockpit with me while I read, but she has this habit of always moving her feet and it's driving me insane, especially because her feet keep touching my leg.

"It's involuntary," she says.

"I know, I know," I say.

"Restless Leg Syndrome," we say in unison. She's been using this excuse for her frantic, always-moving feet forever. I don't think she has an official diagnosis, though.

Dad comes up from the cabin with a tray of Saltines and sliced cheddar. It used to be my favorite boat snack, and it's still Olive's.

"Yay!" she says, like he just offered her the perfect meal.

"Thanks," I say, ignoring the tray and turning back to my book, hoping Dad isn't here to chat. Everywhere I move on this boat, someone follows, and since the day the dinghy got untied, my parents are less inclined to let me use it as a refuge. My little room is the only place where people don't bother me, but even I'm not such a glutton for punishment that I'm going to miss every sunny day this summer.

We're docked near Imperial, Missouri, at Hoppies Marina, which is pretty tiny. Still, I'm glad we're stopped for a while. It's a bit of a catch-22, because if we're sailing, no one really bugs me, but they want my help to, you know, sail. But when we're anchored and I don't have any official duties, everyone wants family time.

Dad and Olive start crunching the crackers really loudly and talking about the next good fishing spot, so I stand up to go. Maybe I can move up on top of the bow and be alone for a while now that Dad's entertaining Olive.

"Clem, where are you going?" asks Dad.

And I know it might be an innocent question, but it feels like a dig to me. *Clem, why do you mope around so much? Can't you sit with the family and have a fun chat about fishing like Olive does?*

"I just want to read."

"Well, you can read here with us," says Olive. "I wasn't bothering you."

"Actually, your feet were," I say. I look at Dad. "I'm just going to go up on top of the bow."

"You can read anytime, Clem," he says. "We're here to spend the days together."

I fold my arms across my chest. He isn't going to let me go. I'm *reading*, for God's sake. Aren't parents supposed to encourage that kind of thing? This is ridiculous.

"You'll be leaving for college soon," says Dad. "You know, we're all going to miss you a lot. Right, Livy?"

My little sister nods up and down, up and down while she crunches her third Saltine cracker. "I'll miss you like the sky misses the rain."

"The sky doesn't miss the rain, Olive," I say, trying to keep my tone measured. "The desert does. Besides, I still have a year at home." I haven't even thought about college—it's light years away. I have to trudge through a whole nother year of everyone hating me and random underclassmen whispering behind my back in the hallways. College may save me, but not for a long, long time.

"I just want to be alone," I continue. "Okay, Dad?"

He frowns, disappointed in me.

Join the club, I think. Then I turn to walk up the starboard side of the boat to find a spot in the sun where it'll be quiet. Or quieter.

But I run into Mom, who's coming down from the bow, where she was Windexing the hatch, to join us for crackers.

"Ooh, they're ready!" she says, blocking my path and staring at the Saltine tray. "Clem, sit down and have a snack."

And that's when I snap.

"Yeah, they're ready!" I say. "Isn't it amazing how Dad can slice cheese and open a package of crackers? It's freaking incredible! He should have his own show on the Food Network about crackers and cheese. You could do all sorts of fun combinations, Dad, like Goldfish and Gruyère or Ritz and Brie or Triscuits and feta! We should just all ooh and ahh over these Saltines with cheddar for hours. In fact, let's do that. Let's sit here, as a family, and marvel at the wonder that Dad has created here with this cracker tray. It's salty and tangy and oh-so-delicious, don't you think, Livy?"

Olive stares at me with wide eyes. I know I'm being crazy now, but I can't stop myself.

"Mom, have one!" I say, grabbing for the tray.

Dad reaches for it at the same time, and when I pull, it doesn't come. Instead, the Saltines go flying into the air, separated from their cheddar slices. It's raining crackers and cheese for a brief moment, and then everything lands on the floor of the cockpit, ruined. On a boat, the five-second rule is no good, because no matter how clean you are, the cockpit floor is always muddy and wet.

"Oh, shit!" I say. "I guess Dad will have to spend a whole *minute* whipping up some more!"

Then I push past Mom and leave my entire family in the cockpit, open-mouthed and surrounded by soggy crackers and dirty cheese.

⛵

When I get up to the bow, I have to bite my lip so I won't start crying. I don't think I'm going to have a peaceful, quiet afternoon after that outburst. I'm not even sure why I did it. I just felt so trapped all of a sudden.

I can't explain anything—my feelings about Ethan, what happened between us, why I'm so angry now. It all seems so vague and intangible. I look out at the water and I'm glad for the sound of the waves and the wind, so I don't have to hear my parents talking about me. I let a few tears fall, but I have to stay quiet. That's one of the hardest parts of being on this boat. I can't even let go and cry without everyone knowing.

chapter twenty

Dear Amanda,
I know you suspected things were weird with
me and Ethan, but it's not as bad as you're
thinking. It was—

Amanda was smart. She could tell something was wrong. She just couldn't guess what it was, maybe because she didn't think it was possible.

One day after school we drove to FroYo-Go, our favorite frozen yogurt spot. I got vanilla with "fresh" strawberries (though they always looked like the prepackaged, syrupy kind to me), and Amanda got her standard peanut butter yogurt with Reese's Peanut Butter Cup pieces on top. We sat in the window and watched cars pull into the strip mall. A few more people from school came in, but no one we knew really well, so we just exchanged a couple of casual smiles.

We were talking about how Henry really wanted to go to this

USC film school summer program, but I could tell that Amanda's mind was somewhere else. I could see in her eyes that she was working out a worry in the back of her head.

So I asked her: "What are you really thinking about?"

And she told me: "I think you've been acting weird about Ethan."

Play dumb, just play dumb. "No I haven't—what are you talking about?"

"I'm not sure what it is," she said. "But I'm not an idiot, Clem. I just *know* there's something that's bothering you about him."

She looked down at her yogurt, stirring it distractedly. Then her tone changed as she said quietly, "I just know it."

I didn't know what to say, so I stared out the window for a minute. My heart was pounding and I wondered if she could hear it. Can people hear hearts?

But then I knew what I had to do, and even though I didn't want to, I did it: I got mad. And I mean really mad. I reacted hugely.

"Amanda, I'm sick of you bugging me about this!" I hissed. I tried to keep my volume low, but the tone attracted stares anyway. Amanda looked up at me, her face surprised.

"I'm not jealous that you have a boyfriend!" I stated, and I knew we had an audience. "Not officially, not unofficially, not secretly, not even subconsciously. It's only in *your* mind! And if you ask me, it's a little weird that you spend so much time thinking about it."

Her eyes looked hurt, and she slowly walked over to the trash can and threw away the rest of her yogurt. I followed, slamming my cup into the garbage and walking out without looking to see if people were watching. I stepped into the chilly spring air and went to the passenger side of Amanda's car. When I got in, she turned up the radio to fill the silence.

I tried to stay in the character of the annoyed friend who

didn't like being called jealous because she'd never really had a boyfriend at school. I could feel my lip quivering a little, so I turned my head to the window.

By the time we got to my driveway, Amanda had something to say.

"Okay, Clem," she said, as I reached for my door handle. I was trying to keep up my mad stance, but the truth was that inside I was about to crumble. I held my face still and looked over at her. "I believe you," she said.

"You do?" I asked.

"I do," she said. "I'm so sorry. We've talked about it before, and I shouldn't have brought it up again after you told me you were fine and not feeling jealous or left out or anything."

I nodded, trying to keep my mouth straight and solid. *Don't quiver.*

"I guess I just thought I saw something the other night, or I thought I saw the way you looked at him, like he worried you," she continued. But then I watched her face change as she pushed those memories out of her mind. She erased them so that she could believe in me.

"But I was wrong," she said. "And I'm sorry. I really am."

She unbuckled her seat belt to give me a sideways hug, and I sat there, a little stunned and unsure. Amanda must have thought I was still mad because, mid-hug, she said, "Oh, come on! Forgive me already!"

And then I let my arms go around her, too, and we were hugging, best friends, all okay, all smiles. Right before I got out of the car, I saw a flicker of doubt cross her face again.

"Clem?" Her voice was tentative.

"What?" I asked, anger gone, just fear in my face now. She knew. She knew I was covering it up.

"Nothing," she said. "See you tomorrow."

"See you tomorrow." I left her car and went inside, ignoring Olive's "Clem? You home?"

I had to get to my room, where I could write in my journal, jot it down, figure it out. And try to justify lying, bold-faced, to my very best friend, who absolutely knew that something wasn't right.

chapter twenty-one

I wake up to the sound of a foghorn, which is about the loudest honk that exists in the world. If you've never heard one, consider yourself lucky. It's not a nice way to face the morning.

I pull the covers over my head, to no avail—Olive's scampering feet are coming to get me. I hear them like you can hear zombies outside the door in one of those movies about the end of the world.

"James is here!" she bellows, ignoring all etiquette and throwing open my door with the energy of a Disney character.

"Huh?" I grunt. One plus of being on a boat is that people really can't drop in on you, seeing as how you're surrounded by water most of the time. We spent last night anchored out in the river—not at a marina—so there's no way James is here.

"He came over in his dinghy," says Olive. "He's having a hot chocolate with Mom and Dad in the cockpit!"

I sit up and peer out of my small window. Sure enough, there's the motor-powered dinghy from *Dreaming of Sylvia*—which is called *Little James*—tied to the side of our boat. I pause for a second and think, *Awww*. But then I remember that I'm annoyed at him for being here.

"Olive!" I say. "What does he want?"

"He wants to go exploring," she says. "He's going to take us on a morning ride before we get underway. Dad said we could."

I fall back into my bed and pull the covers up again, but Olive is right in my face, dragging them off of me.

"Fine," I say, giving in. "Let me get dressed."

I shoo her out of my room.

Olive bounds out the door and up the cabin steps while I survey my face in the small mirror hanging near my bed. It's not good. In fact, it's at least orange-alert-level puffy. After the cracker incident yesterday, I pretty much spent the rest of the day and night strategically avoiding everyone in my family. This is no small feat on a forty-two-foot boat, trust me. I don't really care if my family can tell that I've been crying. They probably know that anyway, seeing as how Mom didn't even bother me about coming to dinner—she let me sneak a bowl of cereal back to my room. But I don't want James to know.

I think of a few impossible options, like putting cucumbers over my eyelids for five minutes or rummaging through Mom's toiletries to see if she has eye de-puffer. It's not likely. Besides, the more time I take getting ready, the more it seems like I care what I look like in front of James. Which I don't. But can you blame a girl for not wanting to go out looking like she's gone ten rounds with the Kleenex box? James already drew me with sad eyes; I don't want him thinking I'm a total shipwreck. Even if I am.

I put on my bathing suit, which is what passes for a bra and underwear during a summer of boating, and a pair of cotton shorts. I throw on a T-shirt, too, so my shoulders won't burn too badly. I grab some sunscreen and am about to head above deck when I have a stroke of brilliance.

Sunglasses. I grab the dark oval ones that make me feel like Audrey Hepburn and put them on even before I see a hint of sunlight. These will hide my eyes until they de-puff.

Dad's in the kitchen making eggs, and Olive is refilling hot chocolate mugs with fresh boiling water.

"Good morning, Clementine," says Dad, mussing my hair. He's trying.

"Morning," I say. I'm trying too.

"Here," says Olive, handing me a steaming mug filled with big marshmallows. She smiles at me with all her teeth.

"Thanks."

When I step out of the cabin, I see Mom throwing her head back and laughing at something James said.

"What's so funny?" I ask.

I have to admit, it's freaking gorgeous out. It's only 8:30 a.m., but the sun is in full swing and the water is sparkling like it's filled with floating diamonds. I sit next to Mom.

"Hey, Clem," says James. "I just came over to see if you and Olive wanted to go for a ride in the dinghy. Dad's taking care of some things today, so I thought I'd get out of his way and spend the morning somewhere else."

"Oh yeah?" I say. I want to ask him if his dad's okay, but somehow that moment where I saw Mr. Townsend crying felt so private that I hold back.

Olive pops up with a plate of eggs for James, and then goes back down to get more.

"I didn't mean to invite myself to breakfast, but if someone's making it, I'm eating it," says James.

"Rob will be thrilled that someone outside of the family gets to try his famous scrambled eggs," says Mom.

"Just remember to rave," I say.

Olive brings up two more plates, and then she and Dad join us outside. James compliments the eggs just enough to sound sincere, but not over-the-top. I watch him tell my parents about how yesterday his dad got in a conversation with another boater, and they used bullhorns to yell back and forth until a third boater with his own bullhorn told them to "Shut up!"

"Dad just waved at the third boater and said, 'Well, hello there! Fine day, isn't it?'" says James. "The guy had no choice but to smile back."

He talks about his dad with such admiration—he's beaming through this whole story. My parents are laughing, Olive is riveted, and I'm just watching the way James's mouth turns up, so easily, so quickly.

This guy is in touch with some deep inner happiness.

Mom and I take everyone's plates downstairs, and I offer to help clean up, but she says, "Go on, go have fun."

So I do. Olive and I grab life jackets and lower ourselves into James's dinghy with two fishing rods and a bottle of sunscreen.

As we pull away from *The Possibility*, the boat sputters and makes crazy noises.

I look at James sideways, but he just laughs and pounds on the motor. "*LJ* purrs like a kitten, right?" he says. Then he lets out a huge laugh that makes Olive giggle. I have to admit that James's joy is kind of contagious.

James waves to my parents in the cockpit. Then he turns to us and says, "Where to?"

"Uh, left?" I say.

"Port it is!" says James, steering the boat around the bend in the cove where we'd moored. We motor by a private swimming dock where a mother and her toddler are sitting on a blanket in the sun, we pass a great blue heron standing on its long, thin legs near the shore where it's fishing for breakfast, and we come across a couple in a double kayak who wave hello.

When we turn around a second bend, Olive points to a fallen tree and shouts, "Fishing hole!"

James eases off the sputtering motor and we drift toward the spot.

Olive immediately opens up the tackle box and chooses a lure shaped like a tiny plastic frog. She expertly sets it on the hook and casts toward the tree.

I see James watching her, impressed.

"Total pro," I say to him.

He smiles. "Do you fish?"

"Sometimes," I say. "I like it, but I'm not, like, *really* into it."

"Same here," says James. "And I'm bad at unhooking wet, floppy things, so you're on your own, Olive."

Olive pays no attention to us—it's like she didn't hear him. She's big on concentration.

I start to feel awkward, like I'm going to have to talk to James for an hour or something while my little sister sits there robot-fishing, so I open up the tackle box and look at the lures to occupy myself. There's a hard plastic fish that's silver and blue, some glittery green worms, and these crazy rainbow jigs that look like mini pom-poms.

I'm about to pick up one of the pom-poms when James asks, "Are you having a good summer?"

It feels like a casual question, one that anyone would ask when they first meet someone else, but I'm still not sure how to answer.

I could go with, "Great! How about you?" or I could say, "Yup,

115

it's fun to hang out with my family," or I could say, "Not really. I'm actually having a pretty hard time with things right now."

But right, like I'd choose option three. I go with "Yup, it's fun to hang out with my family," because it sounds less fake and blow-offy than "Great!"

"Yeah, I like being with my dad," says James. "Guy time."

He flexes his biceps in mock machismo and I grin. He's totally skinny, but he does have some tight arms.

"Do you guys do this every summer?" I ask.

I think I see a shadow cross his brow—the first darkness on his face ever—but it's gone in a split second and I can't be sure I saw it, because he's back to his default state: smiley.

"We've done it since I was thirteen," says James. "So, for the past four summers."

"You're seventeen?"

"Yeah," he says. "You?"

"I turned sixteen in June," I say.

"Did you get your license?"

I nod. "Yeah, it's ironic—right when I got my license, I gave up my freedom to be stuck on a boat with my entire family."

"But you said you like time with them," he says.

"Well, yeah, but not *constant* time like I'm getting."

"That's what the dinghy's for."

"I guess."

"No, but seriously, I think of the boat as my freedom," he says. "Out on the water with the wind blowing through the sails . . . it feels like flying."

"Unless your mom is yelling at you to untie the ropes and your dad is shouting 'helm's alee' or some other nautical jibberish," I say. "Sometimes I wish I could get in a car and drive away for a while."

"Nah." James shakes his head. "You're wrong. Being out on the water is the best feeling in the world. So much better than just driving with the windows down."

I flash back to the country drive with Ethan, and suddenly I'm picturing it all over again—"Beautiful Girl," his hand on mine over the shifter, lying back in the tall grass . . . Amanda on the porch. I grab the side of the boat to steady myself.

"Whoa, you okay?" asks James.

"I'm fine," I say, too quickly.

Olive looks at us then, and I know she's paying attention; she heard the *not*-fine tone of my voice.

I smile at her halfheartedly. She frowns.

"Do you want to go back?" she asks. I feel like I might cry. Again.

I shake my head no, and as I will myself to stare at the fishing lures one more time—red, yellow, blue—I push Bishop Heights out of my head. I'm here, on the water, far away from all of that. I'm okay.

"Want to hear a joke?" asks James. He's smiling warmly at me.

"What?" I ask, still feeling slightly disoriented.

"A joke. You know, to make you smile again."

"Sure!" says Olive, reeling in her lure and looking up at James attentively.

"Okay, this isn't mine—it's from my favorite comedian, Mitch Hedberg. He died, but I can't stop telling his jokes."

I nod.

"Wait—you guys have seen Pringles, right?" he asks.

"Pringles?" I ask.

"The potato chips," he says.

"Uh, yeah," I say. *Duh.*

"Okay, cool. So here goes," says James.

Olive looks up at him expectantly.

"I think Pringles is a really chill company," he starts. "Their original intention was to make tennis balls, but on the day the rubber was supposed to show up, a truckload of potatoes came instead. Pringles is so laid back they just said, 'Whatever. Cut 'em up!' "

I try to suppress a grin, but I can't. I have always thought Pringles cans looked like tennis-ball holders. I give James a small, but real, smile.

Olive holds her stomach because she's laughing so hard.

"Overkill, Livy," I say.

"What will it take to make you laugh out loud?" James asks me.

"Clem used to laugh all the time," says Olive. "She used to be funny and bubbly and bright and—"

"Olive, enough." My tone is firm—James doesn't need to know how I used to be. Or why I'm not that way anymore.

"She still seems like all of those things," says James. "If you catch her unaware."

I look at him sideways and resolve to *not* let him catch me "unaware."

James drops a fishing line in then, and he and Olive keep casting, getting a few nibbles but no real bites over the next hour or so. They ignore me, but in a way that respects the quiet nature of the day, I guess. Like they know my thoughts are complicated right now.

I watch the waves come in, watch a tiny bird on the shore hopping around and looking for washed-up clams, watch the kayaking couple go past us one more time.

While I'm still, I think about all the things I'd like to talk to James about. The old me would ask him how he got into drawing, what his land life is like, which bands he likes, what TV he DVRs, and maybe even if he has a girlfriend.

Olive's right. I used to be brighter.

I feel like a dull and worn-out version of myself, and for some reason I just can't bridge the gap between who I used to be and the sad sack that's sitting here now. I don't know how to reach through it.

I'm staring down at my left thumb, picking at the skin around the nail, when James says my name.

"Clementine."

He sounds like Ethan when he says it. Why can't I just go back and *not do* what I did? Then Amanda and I would be *dying* over being apart this summer, and I could save up stories for her about how my mom is making us eat from a can every night and my dad is being supercheesy and Olive is trying to discuss literature with me. Maybe I'd even tell her about today, about James. Because then meeting him would be this uncomplicated, fun thing. Not that I think he's in love with me or anything, but let's face it, we're out on the water. The pickings are slim.

But I can't even talk to Amanda. Because I'm a bad person.

I look up at James and have to shake my head for a minute to remember where I am. I bite my bottom lip because, for the hundredth time this summer, I feel like I might cry.

"What happened?" he asks.

"Nothing," I say, faking a smile. "I guess I just zoned out for a sec."

I look over and see that Olive is watching us.

"No," he says. "Not just now. I mean, what happened to you?"

"What happened to me?" I echo.

"Did something—" he starts. Then he looks at Olive and sees her listening to us. He holds back. "I mean, I know what it's like to have something make you sad."

"No, it's nothing," I rush to answer again.

"You just looked like—"

"You don't really know me," I say, annoyed at how much he sees. That drawing of me with the sad eyes—what was that supposed to be? And now he thinks he can read my expressions? So presumptuous. "We just met."

James looks hurt for a moment, and then he glances at Olive. I glare at her to let her know that she'd better not butt in with whatever crazy version of the Ethan story she thinks she knows.

She stays quiet, and I look down at the bottom of the dinghy with its dirt scuffs and brown pools of water, wishing I could bubble up and be the old me again. But I don't know how.

chapter twenty-two

Dear Amanda,
On my birthday, it wasn't what you thought—

The day I turned sixteen was a teacher workshop day, so I spent the morning at the DMV and passed my test with flying colors. Dad handed over the keys instantly. "Go have fun," he said.

I dropped him off at home and sat in the driver's seat as I texted all my friends to see who could hang out with me.

The first reply came from Ethan: I'm in. come get me.

I waited exactly twelve minutes, by the clock on the dashboard, to see if anyone else would answer. They didn't. I felt a small thrill at the thought of picking up Ethan and driving around with him, alone.

He was standing in his driveway when I got there. His hair was wet from the shower. I wondered if he had taken one after I texted, if he was clean just for me. When he got in the car he smelled fresh, like Old Spice and spearmint gum.

It was a sunny day and the temperature was in the seventies, so we rolled down the windows and took a left on Rural Route 102. You take a right to go into town; there's no real reason to go left—it just leads to a narrow stretch that passes some farmland out in the county, and eventually it becomes a dirt road. But Ethan hadn't been out that way, and it's pretty in some parts. It seemed like a good idea.

The road was fun to drive, too—lots of valleys and views.

"Do things look different from the driver's seat?" asked Ethan as we dipped down a hill. I could see cows in a field ahead, and I remembered coming out here on a field trip in first grade. Amanda and I got to give a bottle to a newborn calf.

"They do," I said. "I feel like I'm actively involved in the landscape, rather than just watching it go by."

And I realized as I said it that that's what being with Ethan felt like. Like I wasn't watching and waiting for something to happen, for someone to notice me, for life to come my way. I was participating in life. I was making decisions.

"No song game today?" asked Ethan, teasing me.

I had my iPod plugged into the radio jack, but we were listening to a Bon Iver album straight through.

"We could put on one of your playlists," I said, kind of excited about the idea of listening to his playlist *with* him.

"No fair," he said. "Then all the songs are how I feel about you, and none are how you feel about me."

Right then, I felt the day going from exciting but ordinary birthday to the possibility of *more*. But more what? It wasn't like when we went to the movies, where we nervously laughed and brushed hands and flirted, or even when I sat on the couch watching Spike Lee and let his hand touch mine. This felt bigger.

I considered turning back, saying I only had the car for an

hour, making up an excuse about having to meet Amanda later. I thought about reminding him of his girlfriend, bringing up the conversation we had at Razzy's again.

But it almost felt like we were driving in our own world—like we were inside a snow globe—and there was music and sunlight and smiles and laughter floating in the air. And it was all self-contained in a beautiful bubble filled with glittering water that made things seem a little unreal, a little dream-like and hazy. I'm sure the Bon Iver album helped.

It was amazing to be with Ethan this way. I didn't want to break the spell.

I shifted into third gear as we went down a steep hill, and I pushed the rest of the world from my mind.

"I love that you can drive stick," said Ethan. "It's hot."

I smiled at him, and he put his hand over mine on the shifter. I didn't move my hand until I had to shift back into fourth when the road leveled out. We kept talking this way, and the farther we got from town, the more it felt like *we* were the couple, not he and Amanda.

There was a pause in conversation as Ethan clicked through the iPod, looking for a playlist after the album ended. He landed on "Beautiful Girl," and we listened to it in silence together. I hoped he couldn't see that I had goose bumps.

We drove until we got to the dirt road, which was about forty miles from the turn we took. Aaron and Amanda drove out here for one of our scavenger hunts—"dust from the dirt part of Rural Route 102" was on the list, and even though Aaron wanted to just pick up any dirt and pass it off as *the* dirt, Amanda didn't like to cheat.

"He said no one would know where the dirt was from," she'd told me later.

"No one would have," I'd said. "You guys could have won." My team with Renee had just beaten Amanda and Aaron that night, 42 to 41.

"I would have known," she'd said, sure that I would understand. "It wouldn't have felt like winning."

I slowed the car and looked out the window at the dirt road.

"What's past this?" asked Ethan.

"I have no idea," I said.

"We should definitely find out." He smiled at me in a way that made my heart buckle. I thought he might kiss me later, when we stopped driving. And I wanted him to, so badly.

At first the dirt road continued just like normal 102, past farmland and the occasional trailer. But then, as we rounded a slight bend, we came to a dead end. There was a road turning to the right, but it was blocked by an orange construction sign.

"Should we drive past it?" I asked. I was sure I could maneuver Mom's Honda around the edge of the sign, and I didn't want to turn back. I felt like turning back would be a big wind-down of this fantasy day with Ethan. *Not yet*, I thought.

"Maybe we can just park and check out the fields," said Ethan. "It doesn't look like anyone's around."

"Okay," I said. I was sad to leave the playlist behind—I was worried the car was my snow globe and it would shatter without us being in this small space filled with music and sunlight.

It turned out, though, that the snow globe was bigger than I'd imagined. We high-stepped through grass that hadn't been mowed all spring, where blue and yellow wildflowers were growing. When we found a shady spot near a lone tree in the middle of the field, Ethan smoothed out some grass and said, "Let's sit."

I sat down, legs stretched out in front of me, and he lay next to me, his elbow propped under his arm and his face turned in my direction. He handed me a tiny cluster of wildflowers that he'd picked along the way—I hadn't even seen him do it.

"Thanks," I said shyly. It felt like some old-fashioned courting ritual, us sitting under a shady tree in the middle of a farmer's field.

I got nervous then.

"Did Amanda ever tell you about how in first grade we came out somewhere near here and met baby cows? We even got to give one of them a bottle, and it was so cute and—"

Ethan put his hand on my thigh. I stopped talking.

Then he whispered, "Clementine." It was a sigh. I knew nothing was going to follow it. He wasn't starting a sentence, he was just saying my name. He said it reverently, like he liked the sound of it in his mouth.

I lay down next to him, careful not to touch him, though he kept his hand on my leg. It felt like we were the only two people in the world at this moment. We lay there for hours, until we were in the sun after the shade had changed its position, and we just talked. It was easy. It was *Ethan*. We compared the nerdiest things we'd ever seen: I once witnessed this kid Ron Jenson typing "Sent from my iPhone" into an e-mail on his laptop.

"He does *not* have an iPhone," I said.

Ethan countered that in his old town he knew someone who refused to use a mouse—ever.

"He knows all the key commands and proclaims that anyone who uses a mouse is a total caveman," he said.

I laughed, but insisted that Ron's fake iPhone was worse.

"Agreed," said Ethan.

It was just so *normal*. Like we were together. It felt like the rightest thing I'd ever known. But it wasn't. Not even close.

chapter twenty-three

"More cheese!" shouts Olive.

We're dumping a whole pack of shredded cheddar on top of the burrito-like casserole dish Mom's making.

I've been force-recruited into helping with dinner tonight, because Mom decided it was time for me to "snap out of it," at least for the evening. After this morning with James, I feel sunkissed and confused. I went out on the dinghy expecting a couple hours of small talk and jokes, but then talking to James made me think of Ethan. How messed up is that?

Dad has been alternating between reading the newspaper he picked up at the dock deli yesterday and laughing at me, Mom, and Olive in the kitchen, surrounded by empty cans.

"It takes all three of my girls to make one *Man, Can, Plan* dish," he says, smiling.

Mom reaches over and bats him on the head with her oven mitt.

He stands and puts his hands on his hips, pretending to be mad, but then he just picks her up into a hug and twirls her around. I roll my eyes at Olive, and she does the same back to me.

"You guys are cheesier than this," says Olive, and she points at the layer of cheddar we just added to the bean casserole dish.

"Just showing you guys how true romance is done," says Dad, setting Mom down gently and giving her a kiss on the mouth.

"Yeah," I say. "It's so romantic being in a forty-two-foot space with your two kids and eating your weight in canned beans."

"You're looking at it all wrong, Clem," says Mom, taking my hand and guiding me to the port window, practically dancing. She points outside. "What do you see?"

The dark waves are lapping against the boat, and there are sparkling lights on the shoreline in the distance. It looks ordinary and extraordinary all at once. We're on a boat, spending summer on the water. But I'm also bored half the time, and if I'm not bored I'm sad.

When I don't say anything, she asks, "See the water out there?"

"I'm not blind," I say.

"It's blue and cold and wonderful, and it's gently rocking us as we make a family dinner," she says.

"Are you about to break out in song?" I ask.

"No," she says, putting her arm around me and turning me back to face Dad and Olive in the kitchen. "I just want you to see out there, where it's blue and wild and full of adventure. And then I want you to see in here, where there's a warm yellow glow and your family is making dinner and your mom and dad are dancing and your little sister is hoping that you'll throw a smile her way. This is the good stuff, Clem."

"Now that the Hallmark commercial is over, can we put that dish in the oven already so dinner will be ready by bedtime?" I ask.

I understand what Mom is trying to do, but I'm so not in the mood.

I start heading to my room, but Dad stops me.

"I just want to grab the e-reader," I say.

"As long as you read it out here," says Dad.

"Fine."

I get the e-reader and sit down at the end of the couch. Olive pushes in next to me and looks up at my face while I'm trying to read.

"I'm trying to read."

"Can you braid me?" she asks.

This is how she always asks me to fix her hair, even if she means two ponytails or just a brushing—she always says "braid me."

She holds up the brush in her hand.

"A real braid, please," she says.

"Your hair's too short," I say, not looking up from the novel.

"Not for a little one," she says. "Pleeeeease, Clem?"

I sigh and put my reading aside. Then I take Olive's shoulders and turn her around so her back is to me. I collect three short pieces of hair and make a tiny braid.

"There," I say. "You've got a braid."

I'm reaching for the reader when she says, "More, please."

I sigh and start again, taking three more short pieces and turning them into a second braid, then repeating. By the time dinner's ready, my little sister has near dreadlocks. But she looks insane instead of cool. She runs to the mirror in her room, though, and comes out smiling like I've just made her ready for the red carpet.

"I love it," she says, and she puts her arms around me. "I look like a rock star."

"One of the crazy ones," I say, patting her back.

"Those are the best kind," she says as she pulls out of the hug, and I can't help but smile at her unique, secure sense of who she is. She'd probably wear those braids outside if Mom let her.

We sit down to dinner, and I feel okay for a little while. Olive shakes her head around, showing off her wild braids, and Mom and Dad talk about the rest of our route and how we'll be able to go swimming soon when we get to a spot where the currents aren't so strong.

Dinner ends up tasting decent, and Olive says it's because of the cheese we added. Mom admits that she doesn't love cooking, even though she volunteered for the position, and she looks at me pointedly.

"I don't want to cook," I say, pulling four pudding cups out of the mini fridge for dessert.

I sit back down and pull the seal off my pudding. Then I lick the top.

"I think it would be a nice thing to do," says Dad. "Maybe you could relieve Mom every other night."

"It would be a nice thing to do," I say. "But that doesn't mean I'm going to do it."

"What *do* you want to do, Clem?" asks Olive, sticking her spoon into her pudding cup so it stands straight up. She looks at me, and her crazy braids make her seem angry.

"Nothing," I say, not wanting to get any further into this conversation, which suddenly feels too charged.

"Well, you're already doing that every day," says Mom.

She's smiling, but she's not happy.

"Why are you all on my case?" I ask.

Mom and Dad look at each other, and Olive keeps staring at me, her eyes hard. She hasn't even started eating her pudding, and I know chocolate-vanilla swirl is her favorite.

I give her bug eyes back to let her know that I don't appreciate the staring.

"You're not Clem anymore," she says quietly. Then she takes her spoon and starts eating slowly.

"What?" I ask her.

"You've changed," she says, pronouncing "changed" like it's a distasteful word not fit for her mouth.

I stand up and throw my crumpled napkin on the table.

"Olive, you don't even understand what happened to me this year," I say, trying to fight back tears. I can't believe my little sister is getting to me like this, but I feel like I'm about to explode.

"I know what happened," she says. "Something with Amanda."

"Oh, I'm glad you have such in-depth understanding of the situation," I snap.

"Does it matter?" asks Olive. "What's happening now is that you're like a big dark piece of thunder over our whole summer when you're supposed to be fun. You're supposed to be *Clem!*"

"Thunder is a *sound!*" I shout back at her.

I look at Mom and Dad, but they're just quietly eating pudding like they're watching this scene on TV or something, like I'm their evening entertainment.

"Aren't you going to say something?" I ask Dad.

"She's right," he says.

"Oh, well, I guess I'll just change my mood and my entire emotional being to accommodate you guys," I say, my voice dripping with sarcasm. "Yeah, that's it, I'll just flip the happy switch and forget about the fact that I'm a terrible, deceptive person who has no friends and who doesn't deserve a minute of happiness this summer!"

By the end of my shout, my voice has gone high and started to crack. I didn't expect this.

Mom stands up and reaches out to hug me. "You don't think that," she says. "You don't really think that?"

And then I start to cry. I put my hands over my face, but I don't retreat into my room for once. I know they'd just follow me in there anyway, and it's crowded enough as it is in the main cabin. There's no way to get away from my family, so they might as well see me, see how I'm feeling, take a good long look at the wreck of a person I am inside.

I cry for what feels like an hour in that heaving, gushing way that spills onto everything around us. First it's Mom's shoulder, then it's Dad's sleeve as he reaches to hand me a napkin. Finally, it's Olive's braided head as she joins the family hug-huddle and a ball of snot drops from my nose.

It's so incredibly gross, but it makes me giggle through a sniffle as Olive steps back.

"Snothead," I say, embarrassed and feeling weak but relieved, like something came out of me just now, and not only a green glob.

"Clem, you know we love you so much," says Mom.

"We do," says Dad. "And you're not a bad person. You're just trying to figure out who you are."

"Believe me," says Mom. "If this thing with your friends is the worst thing you ever do, you will have lived a very saintly life."

I shrug. It's hard to believe your own parents sometimes. They don't even really know what happened.

"I will always love you," says Olive, who has to join in with her own proclamation.

"Thank you," I say, and I sigh a big breath.

I think I just let a little bit of what happened go. And it felt good.

chapter twenty-four

"Whatcha readin'?"

I look up and see James standing in front of me, blocking my sun. He's wearing a dark green polo shirt and tan shorts. His legs are superlong, but his calves are somehow both skinny and muscular. His boat shoes must be a size 20 or something. They are *huge*. And yes, I did just give him a full body scan. But I was discreet.

"*Beloved*," I say, glancing down at the e-reader screen. "It's on the summer reading list for school."

"Ooh," he says. "You must go to a good school. We don't have a summer reading list."

"I guess," I say.

"Do you hate it or love it?" he asks.

"What?" I ask.

"Your school," he says. "Your summer reading list."

"I guess I'm indifferent," I say.

"You're doing a lot of guessing today," says James. "Can I sit down?"

"I guess," I say, smiling up at him.

I'm actually glad he's here. We're docked near Paducah, Kentucky, and it's the Fourth of July. Mom, Dad, and Olive went on a mission to find groceries and sparklers, which meant they had to walk a mile into the main part of the town. I opted to stay here, on the dock, and read. For once, no one pushed me to come along—they realized that I need a little space in between all the together time.

James sits down next to me, and his feet hang down, like, half a foot more than mine do over the water.

"You look better," he says.

"I do?" I ask.

"Yeah," he says. Then he holds up his two thumbs and pointer fingers and makes a rectangle to peer through. He frames my face with it, just like Henry did when we were making his movie last year.

"Why are you doing that with your hands?" I ask him.

James doesn't move, just looks at me. "Sometimes to really see something, you have to reframe it," he says.

"What do you see?" I ask.

"Your mouth is relaxed, like it might even smile without any effort from you."

I grin.

"There we go!" he says. "I knew it."

"Well, maybe I had a good last few days," I say.

"Maybe you're getting into the rhythm of sailing life," says James. He looks out at the waves that are rolling in to lap against the dock. "You know, the tides going in and then out, the wind blowing east and then west, the high of a perfect day out on the water, the low of a thunderstorm or a wind that won't go your way."

As he talks, his hands move fluidly to express each condition in some sort of nature pantomime. It makes me laugh.

"Oh my gosh!" he says. "Did Clem Williams just LOL?"

"Please do not use abbreviations like 'LOL' in out-loud conversation," I say sternly.

"I know," he says. "OMG, I can't believe I just did that."

I frown harder, trying not to crack up.

"I did it again!" he says. "This is just OOC."

I laugh. "Okay, you have to stop," I say.

"For you, my darling," he says, "Anything."

"Ooh," I say. "Please also stop with the 'darling' thing. If you start singing the song, I'll stand up and leave."

"Okay, first, I wasn't referencing any song," says James. "And second, where will you go? We're on a dock surrounded by water, and I'm guessing you don't have the authority to man *The Possibility* alone."

"You've got me on number two, but I know for a fact you were referencing the 'Oh My Darlin'' song," I say. "Everyone does that with me. I get it, it's natural, my name is Clementine. No problem. Just don't sing it."

"Actually, I thought of a different song when you told me your name," he says.

"Oh really?" I ask. "What song is that?"

"It's an Elliott Smith song," he says. "It's fantastic, and it suits you."

I'm surprised. I'm intrigued. I have to look up this song later! But I'm not going to tell James any of that. So I just say, "Oh. Cool."

"You're impressed." He fake-pops his collar.

"No," I say. "I'm not."

"It's okay—I can tell. Besides, I'm kind of a music guy, so I know all these songs that other people don't. It's kind of my thing. That's one of the hardest parts about being out on the water, actually— not being able to update my playlists and being out of the loop about new music coming out. I always have to catch up in September."

For a second, I think of Ethan and all of his music, but than I push him out of my mind and say, "Being off-line sucks." As soon as I hear myself say it, I'm not sure it's true.

"I think it's nice, actually."

"Me too."

"But you just said it sucked."

"Yeah, but right when I said it I realized I didn't really think that," I say. "Does that ever happen to you?"

"Yes." James closes his eyes and nods his head, smiling like he knows exactly what I mean. "It's almost like you have to hear it out loud, even from yourself, to realize it's not what you think. It's just what you *think* you think. Maybe because other people would think that way or something. Right?" He opens his eyes and looks at me.

And as roundabout and confusing as what he just said was, I get it. "Right."

"But you and I, we are freethinkers!" He throws two out-stretched hands in the air.

"What is that, the freethinker power gesture?" I ask, reaching up to pull his hands down.

"Don't hate on my freethinker power hands," he says. "What's up with that?"

He holds his palms straight up in the air, and try as I might, I can't get his arms down. I stop trying. He keeps his arms up and looks at me expectantly.

"What?"

"Where's your sense of solidarity?" he asks.

I make a show of rolling my eyes and then I put my arms up in the air too.

"Limp arms!" he shouts. "Get them up there, loud and proud! The freethinkers aren't slouches!"

I push my arms ramrod straight, open my palms to the sun and stare right at him with the most serious face I can muster.

We both crack up and drop our arms.

"Seriously, though," says James. "I do think we need more freethinkers in the world. Be on the lookout."

"Yes, sir," I say, saluting with a smile.

"Make that 'Aye-aye, Captain,'" says James.

"In your dreams," I say. "You're not my captain."

"We'll see about that." James smiles at me like he's half joking, and I feel something light up inside of me.

"What are you thinking about?" asks James.

"Isn't that kind of a girl question?" I regain my composure and try to forget that I just thought about kissing this boy who's less than a foot away from me.

"Isn't that kind of a gender-biased question?" he asks.

"You're right," I say. And then, because I've thought of something to pretend I was thinking about earlier, "I was thinking that I like being off-line because it makes things feel slower, in a good way."

"Totally," says James. "You don't have to keep up, and life goes on even without status updates."

"I know," I say. "People act like they can't live without social networks."

"Well, I act like that most of the year."

"Yeah, me too," I admit. "It just seems so important in real life."

"Real life, yeah," says James.

"But actually," I say, the thought forming as I say the words, "this feels more real to me."

"What does?"

"Being here." I look out at the waves. "On the dock, in the sun, with the sound of the water . . ."

I pause, and I can feel him looking at my profile.

"Hanging out with you," I finish. I almost said "Being with you," but then I played that in my head and it sounded all serious and weird, so I changed it at the last second.

"Thanks," he says. He knocks my knee with his and my skin buzzes where we touched.

Then he starts talking about how the other hard part of boat life is that his dad snores a lot and he used to have trouble sleeping when they first started going on these long boat trips, but now it's like the white noise that helps him sleep.

I laugh. "How does your mom deal with it?" I ask.

As soon as the question comes out of my mouth, I know I've made a mistake. His head drops and he stares at the water, not looking at me at all. It's like his whole body changes.

He sits there like that for a minute, maybe two, hunched over the dock. Just when I think he's going to crumple entirely, he straightens up again and pulls his shoulders back.

"She used to say it was like a lullaby," he says, and he lifts his head up toward the sun and squints really hard like it's hurting his eyes.

"That's nice," I say, thinking that it *is* a nice way to feel about your husband's snoring, and also glad he looks okay again.

James smiles and glances down at his tote bag. He reaches inside.

"Hey, do you mind if I draw?" he asks.

I flash back to the picture of me he sketched—the one where I have such sad eyes.

"I don't want you to draw me," I say, suddenly serious. For-real serious.

"Whoa, egomaniac," he says, laughing at me. "There's a really cool water scene in front of us. I was thinking of sketching that."

"Oh," I say, feeling silly. "Sorry. That was dumb, huh?"

"Nah," says James, looking right into my eyes again. "You're a perfect subject. But later."

"Later?" I ask. "When later?"

"Just later," he says. "Whenever I see you again." Then he turns to the water and zones out, the way I do when I have my journal in front of me and I'm pouring my heart into the pages. He's much less of a spaz than I originally thought.

By the time Olive and my parents get back to the dock, I'm almost done with *Beloved*. James is still by my side, finishing the shading on his drawing. I snapped a phone pic of him—he didn't even notice—and I've been peeking over his shoulder periodically. It's turning out really well. He's capturing the view from this marina perfectly. He started the perspective right from the dock and even drew our shadows in the water. Mine is holding a book, and his is holding a pencil.

"Hi, James!" Olive runs up to us and shows off the Double Stuf Oreos she got to replace the ones we've been snacking on since day one.

I give her a thumbs-up.

"Hey, Olive," says James. "Nice Oreos."

"Were you keeping Clem company?"

"She was keeping *me* company." James looks over at me and smiles.

"It was fun," I say, standing up to wave to my parents, who—as always—are lagging behind Olive. They're each carrying two big eco-bags full of groceries.

"Success!" says Mom as she comes toward us.

"Oh, hi, James." She smiles at him. So does Dad when he reaches us.

"James!" Dad says. "Great to see you."

It's like they were worried that I'd be alone all day brooding and painting my cabin black or something—sheesh.

"Wanna do a sparkler?" asks Olive, her eyes shining excitedly.

"It's not even dark yet," I say, but at the same time, James says, "Yes!"

Olive sticks her tongue out at me and puts down her bag. She roots through it and pulls out a box of sparklers.

Mom and Dad drop their bags too. Apparently, this is a family sparkle moment.

We stand in a circle on the edge of the dock, and Dad takes a lighter out of his shorts pocket. As he ignites each of our sticks, pink, blue, and green sparks fly in all directions, and the fizzy noise makes me smile.

James waves his green stick around like a sword, while Olive draws flowers in the air with hers. Mom and Dad touch theirs together in a patriotic toast, but I just keep mine still, watching the pink sparkles effervesce, burning down to the bottom.

When we're done, Olive cheers "Happy Fourth of July!" and James gives her a high five.

I love how nice he is to her.

"Olive, come help unload," says Mom, picking up her grocery bags and turning down the dock toward *The Possibility*.

"Can't I stay out here with Clem?" she asks.

"Clem has to come in too," says Dad. Then he looks at me.

"After a few minutes, of course. We'll give you time to say good-bye."

I feel my face flush. Like I need time to say good-bye to James? This is totally embarrassing.

"It's okay," I say, edging past James and standing with my family. "James, I'll see you around, right?"

"If you're lucky," he says, grinning.

I stick out my tongue at him and turn to follow my parents up the dock. Then he calls my name, "Clementine!"

We all turn back—my family is so nosy—and I see that he's holding out his drawing. He ripped it out of the sketchbook.

I walk back toward him.

"Here." He hands it to me.

"Thanks," I say, looking at it again. I love the way our shadows are in the foreground. So still, so quiet, hovering at the edge of the water together.

"This is really good," I say. "How come you're giving it to me?"

"So you'll remember what's real."

chapter twenty-five

I help unpack the groceries when we get back to the boat. The cabinets have these storage dividers in them so that things won't move around when the boat rocks, even if we're on a really big tilt. It's a complex operation to put away the groceries, so Mom and I man the galley while Dad and Olive stand in the living-room area with the bags and take out items one by one to hand to us.

During all this activity, I field questions about James. Mom wants to know how long he was sitting there with me.

"A couple of hours, I guess," I say. "I don't really know."

"What did you talk about?" asks Mom.

Dad hands her the coffee grounds.

"Stuff," I say. "But mostly we were quiet; I was reading and he was drawing."

I glance over at the table where I set down James's picture, suddenly feeling protective of it, like I should have taken it into my room.

Dad notices where I'm looking. "This illustration is excellent," he says, picking it up and holding it out for everyone to see. I know he's a huge fan of art kids at his school, even though they're six years old. He always says that they grow up to be the artistic kids in high school, who are the true thinkers. Well, he says that when he's trying to get me to sign up for art, anyway. "We can frame it and hang it up on the boat if you want, Clem."

"Um, no, Dad," I say, taking the paper from him and putting it in my room, in a drawer, where hopefully even Olive won't snoop. That scene is for me.

"Where's James's dad?" asks Olive when I return to the galley.

"I think he was on the boat," I say. "But James just wanted some land time or something. Someone else to talk to."

"He likes talking to you," says Mom as she opens the small refrigerator and motions to Olive to hand her the perishables. "I can tell."

"Okay, okay," I say. "Can we stop with the family discussion of James? He's cool. We're sort of friends. But who knows if or when we'll see him again."

Truthfully, my heart sinks at the thought that we could possibly go off course or James and his dad could change their minds and head somewhere else. I want us to be sailing on the same route, like it seems like we have been so far. I don't want to give him up.

"I'm pretty sure we'll see James again." My dad wiggles his eyebrows up and down. It's hugely dorky.

This is the moment in a normal house where I would exit the kitchen and make the discussion stop. But I'm here. On a boat. With nowhere to go.

"We'll leave you alone," says Mom, mercifully. "But I'm just saying, it must be nice for both of you to have someone your own age to talk to."

"Hey!" says Olive. "I am an excellent talker."

"That you are, Miss Olive," says Dad. He rubs her hair, which

I notice is getting dirty. Like, dreadlock dirty. But I guess if my parents don't mind, neither do I.

"He must miss his mom this summer," says Mom, looking wistful as she puts a new bottle of olive oil up in the cabinet.

I look from Mom to Dad, wondering what they know about James's mom. They spent some time with Bill Townsend, maybe they have the full story. I don't want to ask them, though. I want to see James again, and let him tell me what he wants to tell me in his own time. It seems fairer that way.

"I'm sure he misses her," I say.

"Sylvia sounds like such a lovely woman," says Mom. "I hope we get to meet her one day."

Sylvia, of course—like their boat name, *Dreaming of Sylvia*.

"Bill told us all about her," continues Mom. "How she works with children in other countries every summer through a nonprofit program, and he and James take this trip together while she's gone. Wouldn't it be fun to hear about all her adventures in South America and Africa?"

"Yeah," I say. "That would be cool."

And I feel relieved, because I realize that I was projecting something awful—like that James's mom was dead! But I read it wrong, and she's just away every summer. He must miss her, but it's not like a tragedy.

I smile.

"Want me to help make dinner?" I ask.

⛵

When I get to my room that night, I can hear fireworks echoing around the lake. We watched them for a while as it turned dark, but there are so many going on that we'd have to stay up till 3 a.m. to see them all. I love the happy *pop, pop, pop*s, though.

I take out my journal so I can record this day, and I start thinking in that deep-inside way that I only really pull off when I'm writing a diary entry. There's one thing that's been bugging me—why is James's boat called *Dreaming of Sylvia* if James's mom skips the trip every year?

When I flip to the next blank page to ruminate some more, I see that there's a piece of paper tucked into the journal.

C, I certify that these are mine. Please return them soon. ♥ *E.*

I stare at Ethan's note for a moment. I press my fingers over the indentations where he pushed down the pen. *He was here.* I tuck it farther back in the journal.

Then I write about the day on the dock. About James and how he made me laugh, and how I even wanted to kiss him in a certain moment. But then we settled into something, sitting there side by side, that felt maybe even closer than a kiss. I keep coming back to what he said to me: "So you'll remember what's *real*."

"That's what today felt like," I write. "Real." And then I change up my style so it's like a poem or something—I do that when I'm feeling all deep—and I write in a stacked tower of words:

Solid.
Tangible.
Fundamental.
True.

Before I close the journal, I flip through and find Ethan's note again. Then I crumple it up and toss it in the plastic bag I'm using for trash.

chapter twenty-six

I put my earbuds in, plug the cord into the computer, and do a search until I find the full track. Then I press Play. I close my eyes while I listen so I can block out this dirty old room with its scuffed white walls and weird posters about employee regulations.

Mom got a signal on her cell last night and decided she needed to check in with the office, so we had to get online today. There's supposedly WiFi at the dock, but none of us could get it to work, so we walked into town and found this little Internet café that looks like it hasn't been used since 1999 or whenever it was that everyone got their own connections at home.

Mom is on the computer next to me, and Dad and Olive are going for ice cream across the street. Olive doesn't care about getting online—and I can tell Dad is enjoying his completely off-line summer.

I came here for one thing: "Clementine" by Elliott Smith.

When I start to listen to it, I like the soft sound of his guitar and the edge of pain in his voice. It's definitely a riff on the original song—he keeps singing "Dreadful sorry, Clementine," and something about things being wrong. But it's got this hopeful sound to it, too, and I love hearing my name in a new song that I hadn't known about. You know how hearing your name in a song can make you swoon just a little bit? Yeah, that's happening.

When I'm done listening, all I can think about is how the song reminds James of me. I pull my iPod wire from my bag and log into iTunes to buy it. I want to listen to it again.

Then I close the browser and stare at the desktop for a minute.

Mom is typing furiously, probably answering, like, two hundred e-mails that have come in from work. She gets this really intense look when she's doing work stuff on the computer. She bites her lip and sighs out loud a lot. I know she's completely in her own world right now.

I open another window and log into Facebook. I have to—I can't help it.

At first I just scroll through my friends' updates. I see Henry, Renee, Aaron. But I don't see anything from Ethan. I look at my friends number: 102. When I left, it was 126. I guess I could have anticipated that, but it still stings.

I know I shouldn't, but I try to figure out who else has unfriended me. Amanda only updates a few times a week, so maybe she's just not on my first newsfeed page. My heart speeds up a little. I scroll to page two. There's still a chance that she's there.

But she's not.

I search for Amanda's profile. We are not friends. I feel a sharp pain hit my chest. I guess I expected some random judgmental people from school to go away, and I guess I understand why Ethan has to, even if he maybe doesn't want to. But Amanda? Amanda was always mine.

My head is spinning, but this is my one moment of

connectivity, so I have to pull it together and see it all. There won't be another chance for a while.

Like a true masochist, I look at Renee's photos. There are a bunch of her and the rest of our friends in a new album called "Summer Nights." I notice a shot where Henry has his arm around her and is leaning into the side of her head, and I wonder if they're finally getting together. And I'm missing it. *Heart pang.*

Ethan is there too. His hair is shorter, like he got it cut for summer, and it looks lighter, like he's outside a lot. He's smiling in each shot; he's having a great time. He's there with Amanda.

I click faster, then move back to thumbnail view so I can find the pictures with him in them. There are a few of him with all of my friends. And that's how I think of it: he's with *my* friends.

How did this happen? Amanda *took him back?*

I click to Amanda's profile and open up her latest album—she doesn't protect her photos. That answers my question. Self-takes of Amanda and Ethan kissing; him picking her up on the shore of Dilby Lake, where Amanda lifeguards every summer; them in downtown Chicago by the Art Institute.

I can't freaking believe they are back together.

Amanda forgave him and not me!

I click to my own profile and scroll for wall posts and messages. There are just notes from a few boring groups I belong to. I see a couple of random "Have fun on the water!" messages from people who don't know me very well.

Aaron wrote, "Don't fall off the boat!"

There's nothing from Amanda or Ethan. Not a wall post, not a whisper. I thought one of them might have written me something explaining, something to tell me how they can have this summer without me, like I never existed, like Ethan didn't do anything wrong. I've been erased.

When I check my private inbox, I see a message from Amanda. At the sight of her name, my heart speeds up. Then, just as suddenly, it stops—or at least it feels like it stops. The subject line says, "BITCH." I don't open it, but I don't delete it, either. I'm frozen.

I look over at Mom, feeling panicky and breakable. She's still in her zone. She doesn't see me. I log off and walk out of the little dirty room and into the fresh air. I see Olive and Dad through the window of the ice cream shop across the street. I turn right and walk to the end of the sidewalk. This isn't a very long Main Street. I walk back to the other end of the street and catch my breath. I swallow the lump in my throat. I wish I had stayed off-line.

I keep pacing for a few more minutes, calming myself down. "It's okay, you're okay," I whisper, trying to remind myself of James and the drawing and being in the moment with the sun and the water and the quiet of the day.

I stare at a bunch of wildflowers growing in the parking lot at the end of the street. *How can she forgive him and not me?* There are yellow, purple, and white flowers growing; they all are really tiny. *Do they even miss me?* I'm reminded of a minifloral pattern that used to be on one of Amanda's skirts when we were little. *If they talk about me, what do they say?* I wonder if the flowers are weeds, and someone's going to pull them out of the ground one day and throw them away, even though they're so pretty. *Does Ethan say terrible things about me?* The flowers look even prettier somehow because they're against this hard, gray concrete backdrop. *Does he make it sound like it was all my fault?* Maybe they're more beautiful because they're struggling to grow in a harsh environment. *Does Amanda hate me forever?*

I turn around and carefully look at the sidewalk as I go, noticing some initials, vg + rs, written in the concrete. I see a chalk-drawn hopscotch game in front of the hardware store.

I want to push Facebook from my mind, but it's still there.

Everyone can tell something's off with me when I walk into the ice cream parlor. I try to arrange my face the right way, I try to slow my breathing, I try to smile. I study the menu intensely. Olive sees it first.

"What's wrong?" she asks.

Mom's done with her e-mail and she's eating maple-flavored ice cream. Olive is crunching the lower half of her waffle cone. Dad's loudly draining the last drops of his vanilla milkshake.

I'm such a damn billboard for my emotions. How do deceptive people do it?

I glance over at the ice cream counter.

"They don't have peppermint," I say.

"They have mint chocolate chip," says Dad.

"Not the same," I say.

Olive looks at me sympathetically. I sit down and join the family ice cream table, ice-creamless.

When we get back to the boat, I need some in-my-own-cabin time. They didn't push me to talk earlier, and no one's asking me to do anything now. Mom starts making dinner, and Olive offers to help. I go into my room and close the door. When I get out my journal, I have trouble starting.

The Facebook stuff is still fresh in my mind, and I write about Ethan and Amanda being back together. When I write about Amanda unfriending me, and how she's spending the summer with Ethan, I let a few tears fall, now that I'm finally in a semiprivate space. But I don't bawl my eyes out like I wanted to when I first saw her album. Family ice cream time helped. The flowers in the parking lot helped. Seeing the boat with the sun setting behind it as I walked toward the dock helped. And thinking about James—and seeing him again soon—helped.

I take his drawing out of my drawer and tape it to the wall next to my bed, just so it'll be there when I need to focus on being in the present. With him, with my family. It's a reminder of what's real.

chapter twenty-seven

Dear Amanda,
I know you don't believe me, but Ethan and
I never hooked up. We never even—

Eventually, out in that field in the county, the sun started getting low in the sky, and Ethan and I both started murmuring about "getting back." I wondered, *What happens now?*

But even though I felt like we could talk about anything and everything, I couldn't ask Ethan that. I didn't even know what I *wanted* to happen.

We drove back to town slowly, right at the speed limit. From the moment we got in the car, though, I noticed that something had shifted—things felt off.

For twenty minutes, we were silent.

"Oh," I said, noticing the gas needle close to *E*. "I should stop for gas."

"I should really get home," said Ethan. "Can you drop me off first?"

"Sure." I faced straight ahead.

Ethan checked his phone. "Shit," he said. "It's dead."

"Mine too." I'd noticed that when we were in the field. "They were probably straining to find a signal way out there."

I looked over at Ethan, but he just frowned and put his phone back in his pocket.

He didn't put his hand over mine as I shifted gears, he didn't tell me a story or make me laugh, he didn't even glance in my direction.

⛵

By the time we got back into town, we weren't even listening to music. Ethan hadn't started up a new playlist after the last one ended. And as we got closer to home, the car got quieter and quieter.

When we pulled into his driveway, it was almost 8:30 p.m., nine hours after I'd picked him up this morning. I wasn't worried about Mom or Dad—I was sure they'd think I was out with Amanda, enjoying my first day as an official driver. But I felt a sense of loss as I drove into Ethan's neighborhood, even before I turned into the driveway and saw them.

Amanda's car was pulled up to Ethan's house, and she and Ethan's mom were sitting on the front porch together. Mrs. Garrison must have made iced tea, because there was a pitcher and a plate of sliced lemons on the small table between them. It was such a nice scene. And it made me feel afraid.

I wondered if something bad had happened to Amanda, if she'd needed Ethan or me for an emergency, but she couldn't find either of us because we were together. I felt guilt gnaw at my stomach, and my face got red and splotchy before I even got out of the car.

But when we stepped into the driveway, they both waved. No, they were just hanging out, waiting for us to get back because they couldn't get through to us.

I'm sure Amanda was suspicious about where we were, but we still would have been in the clear, probably, if it hadn't been for the looks Ethan and I both had on our faces. We were guilty of *something*. Our hair was rumpled, we had that sheen of lusty sweat clinging to us, and our eyes were darting, shameful. We hadn't done anything wrong—not really. But we both knew that we had crossed a line, somehow. And it showed.

I could hardly stutter out a "We were driving on these country roads," as Ethan said, "We got lost," at the same time.

Amanda—who'd been half smiling and only slightly annoyed that we weren't back earlier—looked at me, then at Ethan, then at Ethan's mom, who was standing up to go inside. She knew.

"What's going on, Ethan?" asked Amanda, almost shouting.

She didn't pay any attention to me, even as I looked to her for something—I don't know what. She wouldn't even make eye contact.

I didn't know what to do, but I didn't want to lie about anything. So I panicked. I turned to leave, getting back in the Honda. I didn't look at Ethan, who was walking up on the porch to try to calm Amanda down. I didn't look at Amanda again, but I heard her yelling and I could tell she had started to cry. I'd never seen her lose control like this.

The last thing I heard as I reversed out of the driveway was, "With my *fucking friend*, Ethan? My fucking *best friend*?" And I wished Ethan and I had rolled up the windows on the way back.

⛵

"Can you *believe* her?"

"Someone told me they had sex in a field."

"She did that to her *best friend*."

"Amanda's way prettier."

I zombie-walked through the last three days of sophomore year. We had exams, so everyone was just going from test to test, but still, I felt like a hollowed-out shell of Clem Williams.

My parents knew something was wrong. After I got home from dropping off Ethan and facing Amanda, I pretended to be sick. Mom brought me soup in bed and I tried not to burst into tears in front of her. She knew I'd been crying, though.

Olive asked to come in and watch our favorite ABC Family shows on the TV in my room, but I told her no, that I might be contagious, and she stayed away.

All weekend I slept and cried. I stayed off-line because I was too afraid to see if anything was going around about me, but I checked my phone incessantly. I was sure Ethan was going to call, tell me what happened, tell me what he'd said to Amanda.

But he didn't.

I was even more sure that Amanda would call to at least listen to my side of the story.

But she didn't.

And so on that Monday morning I went through the motions— showering, drying my hair, putting on lip gloss and a little swipe of mascara. Dad made sure I had a good breakfast. "Can't have you taking tests on an empty stomach!" he said. Then he kissed my forehead and headed to work, and Olive and I stayed at the table to finish our eggs. She chattered on about end-of-the-year cupcakes and asked me if I wanted her to bring one home.

"No," I said, moving my eggs around the plate with my fork.

"There's always extra," said Olive. "Cameron Brown's mother makes, like, a gazillion because she's a bored homemaker."

I looked up at Olive.

"That's what Mom says, anyway," she said.

Of course Mom says that. She has lawyer-mom guilt because she leaves early and gets home late and doesn't have time to make cupcakes for Olive's class. "That's okay," I said. "I don't need the sugar."

And maybe because it was the first time I'd met her eyes since the Ethan incident, but Olive suddenly looked at me like she knew—*really* knew—that I was not okay.

I saw what seemed like fear and concern flicker on her face, but then she smiled reassuringly.

"Want to borrow my lucky pen for your exams?" she asked.

"No," I said, grabbing my plate and taking it into the kitchen.

"It might help," said Olive, ignoring my rejection. She walked to the entryway where her backpack was sitting, and I heard her rifling through the pockets.

I leaned back on the kitchen island and tried to steady myself. I had no idea what I would face at school.

"Here," she said, coming into the kitchen with a pink pen. It had a feather on the end of it and looked utterly ridiculous.

"Thanks," I said.

When I got to school, I was gripping the pink feather-pen in my right hand as I walked through the hallways. That's when I heard the whispers. That's when I felt the stares.

I knew instantly that even though no one had called *me* this weekend, there had been a lot of talk. A few people came up to me and said things like "Ethan's a jerk," or "Amanda had it coming," but it's not like that made me feel better. Actually, those comments

155

made me feel worse. Ethan wasn't a jerk, I thought, and Amanda *didn't* have it coming; that remark came from mean girls, mostly. Despite those wincing moments, though, I didn't really feel anything at all. It was like I was watching someone else go through this, watching another girl's life fall apart.

I think Amanda's therapist mom would call it "distancing"— avoiding emotion so I wouldn't have to feel the devastation full on.

I kept my head down, walking through the halls with a hunched back and a protective books-in-front-of-chest stance. But when I saw Amanda's sparkling blue ballet flats coming toward me as pondered where to eat my lunch, I instinctively looked up. I caught her eye. She looked like she'd been crying too.

"Stay away from me," she hissed.

I hunched back down and waited for her to pass.

I ate lunch in the corner of the library, sneaking bites of the sandwich Dad had made for me and feeling thankful that he was on a PB&J kick—I couldn't have hidden tuna fish from the librarian who walked the aisles looking for kids breaking the no-food rule. That was mean of her, I realized. Didn't she know that some people didn't have any other place to eat where they wouldn't be exposed for being alone during the school's social hour?

I stared at the science books in front of me. I had wanted to sit in the fiction aisle, but it was crowded with kids who I guess sat here every day and read through lunch. Maybe that would be my life next year; escaping to another world didn't sound so bad to me.

I was about to get up and head to the biography shelves when I saw the sparkling shoes appear on the tan carpet.

Amanda knew where to find me. She hadn't been ready to see me in the hallway, but now she was approaching me fully prepared.

She said my name when she walked up to me.

"Clem."

"Hi," I said, pushing out the chair next to me with my foot, knowing this was my chance.

But the thing was, I didn't know what to say. I couldn't defend myself. "I like Ethan too" just didn't seem to cut it. It wasn't as if I'd just been through some trauma—like my mom dying or Olive being sick or even a really bad exam grade—and I needed to be comforted and Ethan was there.

I'd thought of all the excuses that might have made my friends cut me some slack, but none of them were real. The truth was that I liked Ethan, and he liked me. We clicked. That's it.

It's a paper-thin reason to start something with your best friend's boyfriend, and I knew it.

I deserved every whisper in the hall, I deserved Amanda's scorn and all the tears I'd shed in my bedroom. I deserved to eat my lunch alone in the library. And I deserved the way that Amanda was looking at me.

But it still hurt. A lot.

"You lied to me," she said.

"I didn't, Amanda," I said. "I swear I didn't."

"I knew something was wrong," she said, standing above me with her arms crossed. "I knew it, and you denied it, again and again."

"There wasn't anything going on," I said. "Friday was just—"

Amanda held up her hand.

"I don't want to know," she said.

"No," I said, tears springing to my eyes. "Amanda, we didn't . . . I mean, I would never—"

"I thought you would never do anything *remotely* like this," she said. "Clem, I believed you." She paused and bit her lip. "I was even happy that you and Ethan were friends. Just friends."

"We were!" I said.

"Until you weren't," said Amanda.

"It was harmless," I said, looking down at the maroon-colored table and betraying what I was saying with the desperate way that I said it.

"Stop lying, Clem!" she shouted, and I saw a skinny guy peek around the shelves to look at us. Amanda glared at him and he disappeared. "Ethan told me about how you've been trying to start something with him all year, how you flirt with him in class, and even at my house while we watched that movie."

"That isn't true," I said, my eyes pleading with her to believe me. "We were all crammed onto the couch, and so maybe my leg was touching his hand, but it was just that we happened to be close, and—"

"Are you even listening to yourself?" asked Amanda, her volume lower now, pure loathing in her voice.

"Amanda, please," I whispered. "I even tried to tell him that I thought we were getting too close. I—"

"You took him on a drive way out in the county for the *entire day* after this year-long back-and-forth that's been going on under my nose, and I'm supposed to believe that *nothing happened*?" Amanda leaned in closer to me, leveling me with her eyes.

I shrank back in my chair. "He just texted me back when I asked who wanted to go for a drive. That was all."

"It wasn't all!" said Amanda, her voice growing louder. "He won't tell me what happened, but I know something did—I can tell. And now I'm stuck in the middle of this mess! I have no idea what to do."

"Trust me," I said. "Amanda, we didn't do anything—"

She was smiling at me, and it made me freeze for a moment.

"You never liked Noah Knight, did you?"

I shook my head no, tired of lying.

Amanda let out an odd laugh that sounded like she was in pain.

"Ethan's saying that you were a big mistake," she said, and I could see the darkness in her eyes, despite her smile. "He's begging me not to break up with him."

I felt a sharp knife in my chest, and I hated myself even more for being upset by what Ethan said about me. I wondered briefly if Amanda was lying, but then I remembered how quiet he got in the car ride home. I shouldn't be surprised; he was never mine. What right did I have to feel hurt that he was abandoning me now?

"Amanda," I said. "You have to forgive me, I didn't mean to—"

"Clem." She silenced me with the intensity of her low whisper. "I can't forgive you."

Tears rushed to my eyes—I couldn't stop them.

She looked at me, and this moment pained her, I could tell. But she kept a smile plastered on her face.

"I'm sorry," she said. "You brought this on yourself."

I closed my eyes and nodded, knowing my face was twisting up into the ugly cry, knowing I'd throw the rest of my sandwich away because there'd be no way to choke it down past the lump of sadness in my throat. Knowing I didn't deserve even the small pleasure of peanut butter and jelly.

I opened my eyes after a moment, and Amanda was gone. She knew I was leaving for the whole summer, and that was the last time I saw her.

chapter twenty-eight

"Unfurl the jib!" shouts Dad. It's the perfect sailing day, and he has Mom, Olive, and me all jumping at his commands this afternoon.

Once we get cruising and we're all sitting in the cockpit together with sodas, I bring up the fact that it's not very girl-power of us to be following a man's bellowed commands. Dad rolls his eyes, and Mom points out that this is practically the only time my father gets to be the boss.

"Usually, the three-to-one girl thing rules," she says.

Actually, she's right. I don't know how many times Dad has had to sit through *The Proposal* instead of *Training Day* (his favorite) on family movie night. Although he and I do team up when it comes to college basketball. What can I say? He went to the University of North Carolina and made me a Tarheel fan, so March is our sacred time.

"Enjoy your day in the sun, Dad," I say. He laughs and tips his captain's hat. He has hardly taken the thing off since we started this trip, though he claims that's a protective measure for his skin.

We spend all afternoon out on the water, and by 5 p.m. we're ready to anchor for the night, so we take down the sails and Dad starts to motor in and out of small inlets until we find a good spot. There are a few other boats near us, but not *Dreaming of Sylvia*, I notice. And I feel a little disappointed that James isn't close tonight. I wonder how far they sailed today.

After a taco dinner (with canned beans, but *woohoo!*—fresh lettuce and tomato) I tell my family that I'm tired and want to finish my book. Both of those things are true, but I also want to write in my journal, so I close the door to my room and lie back on the bed, picking up the pink feathered pen.

I'm getting to the last few pages of this journal, I realize. I may run out of room before summer's over. I go through at least one journal every year. I don't write every day, but when I do sit down with it, the ink flows pretty fast and furious. I'll have to remember to pick up a notebook at the next dock deli. I can't have all my genius thoughts and feelings go unrecorded. As *if*. But I do like writing things down—it helps, somehow, although I always had a hard time getting my friends to understand that.

I flip through to see how many pages I have left.

And that's when I see it: Amanda's handwriting. It's on the second-to-last page. My heart starts beating fast, which is so weird, because why would your heart just start pounding like crazy when you see someone's penmanship? It's not like the handwriting is a tiger that should activate the fight-or-flight instinct, which is exactly what I'm feeling right now. It's insane how bodies physically respond to stuff. All of this is running through one part of my mind while the other part is frantically asking, *When did she write this? What did she write? Did she read my diary? Oh, God, why am I just seeing this now?*

My brain is a split-personality psycho.

⚓

I started this journal at the beginning of sophomore year, last fall. Amanda was there when I bought it at the fancy paper store in the mall.

"Remind me why you need this again?" Amanda asked, as I handed a twenty-dollar bill to the cashier.

"Because some things are private," I said. "Not everything can live online."

"Why don't you just set your profile so that only your best friends can see updates and wall posts?"

"Because, Amanda, hard as it is to believe, some things are even private from *you*," I said. Then I grinned at her and stuck out my tongue.

She laughed and twirled a piece of my hair around her finger. "Impossible, darling, you tell me everything!"

"True," I agreed, walking out of the store with my new $8 so-pretty journal. It had an embossed fleur-de-lis pattern on the cover, but the coloring was a dark red, so it wasn't too frou-frou. I loved it instantly.

We walked around some more, peeking at the GAP sale rack and checking out the new designer collection from the discount shoe store. I stopped by Razzy's to ask my boss Mike for my paycheck, and we walked by the movie theater to see if anything good was playing. No luck, so we got smoothies at the stand in the middle of the mall and sat down on a bench.

"So what is it about the journal?" Amanda asked as soon as we got into prime I'm-watching-you-walk-by-but-not-at-an-angle-where-you-think-I'm-watching position.

I was surprised she brought it up again, like she sincerely wondered why I needed it.

"I don't know," I said. "I guess when I write things down, like, physically, it helps me figure out how I really feel."

"How?" asked Amanda.

"Well, like, if I just write down something about us walking around the mall today, I'll probably blabber on for a few lines," I said. "But then maybe I'll remember that when we went by Razzy's you smiled extra big at Mike and then I'll wonder if you have a crush on him or something."

Amanda slapped my arm.

"I do *not* have a crush on Mike!" she said. "He's, like, thirty!"

"Okay," I said, laughing at her. "But you *did* smile at him today, and I totally saw it."

"So that's what you'd write down?" she asked. "The way I smiled at Mike?"

"It's just an example of how my recollections of the day sometimes lead to insights," I said.

"False insights!" said Amanda, but she was still smiling. Not as big as she did at Mike, though.

"It doesn't matter," I said. "Because they're just my own private thoughts."

"Hmm." She took a sip of her smoothie and contemplated this. "I get it."

And that's all I needed from her. I knew she did get it. She knew me as well as anyone ever had.

⚓

I look down at the journal now, and my hands are shaking as I start to read what Amanda wrote.

Clemmy my love, by the time you get to this page, your diary will be filled with insights (true and false) and stories of our sophomore year at BHHS. I hope you have spoken well of me, and that you have not made a note of me smiling big at Mike, your old-ass boss! I also hope that we've both found the perfect boyfriends this year—hot guys with great hair who worship us the way we deserve to be worshipped. And of course we have straight As and vibrant social lives, and maybe even our own cars, if our parents are generous (or if your paychecks from good ol' Mike have increased). You are my true love, in a friend way, and I am yours forever. xoxoxoxoxoxoxooxoxoxo, A
PS—Want me to make you a smile?

I close the journal quickly so the tears that slip down my face don't mar the purple ink on the page. Amanda's page. She must have written it that day in the mall when I went to the bathroom, or when I was obsessively playing with the new phones at the Verizon store. Sometime when I wasn't looking it just poured out of her, so quickly, so easily, because that's what our friendship was like: Effortless. Fast. True.

I swipe the tears off my face and pound my fist against my bed. It makes a soft thump, but that's as much angry noise as I'm allowed on this tiny vessel without attracting Mom-Dad-Olive attention. I wish I could slam a door or scream out loud or throw something, though, because suddenly I am *pissed*.

How could Amanda do this to me? How could she not even ask

for my side of things after all the years we've been friends? Sure, I did something bad, I broke rules, I made a mistake. But does that mean that she thinks I'm evil? That I'm a terrible person who can never be redeemed after . . . after what? I didn't sleep with Ethan, we didn't even kiss. What was it that we did? Nothing!

And then my emotional pendulum swings back to center and my breathing slows. It wasn't nothing, I acknowledge. It was almost a whole school year of pushing boundaries with Ethan. We may have never acted on our feelings, but those feelings weren't okay to have. And they were being encouraged, every day, by both of us. By me.

My anger turns inward: *Why didn't I stop it? How could I have done something so wrong?*

I fall back onto my pillow, exhausted by confusion.

Olive comes into the room without knocking, which I'm getting used to, and she sits down at my side. I close my eyes, and she takes her hand and brushes my hair back from my forehead with tiny little touches. She doesn't say anything, just keeps moving her hand over my head.

And I wonder how my little sister knows exactly what I need as I drift off to sleep.

chapter twenty-nine

The next morning, I get up early and join the family for breakfast. It's always a little chilly out on the water before noon, so I pull my soft hoodie on over my T-shirt and pajama pants and climb outside.

"Hey, sleepyhead," says Mom. She has her legs stretched out on the cockpit seat, and she's holding a cup of chamomile tea. Her freckles are darkening after all this time in the sun, even though she's still wearing that giant floppy hat. It actually looks kind of good on her, I admit to myself.

"Hi, Mom." I take out my phone and snap a photo of her in the early light.

"Are you getting a signal?" she asks.

"No." I put the phone back in my pocket. "It's just habit to carry it around."

"I'm sorry, Clem," says Mom. "You must feel pretty disconnected, huh?"

"Not really."

I ease onto the seat across from Mom and accept the cup of

hot chocolate with big marshmallows that Olive hands up to me from the galley. As I take the first sip, edging one marshmallow out of the way and being careful not to burn my tongue, I see the sunlight sparkling on the water as seagulls dive in to catch their fishy breakfasts. The wind makes the sails bang around, and when the rigging vibrates it creates this sound that I've always thought of as the boat wind chime. I lean back in my seat and peek inside to see Dad just getting the pan out to make eggs. And somehow family breakfast seems like a really nice idea.

⛵

After eggs, Olive and I jump in the river.

"Do not splash me in the face," she says.

This is a big rule with my sister. She hates water in her eyes. I think it's because she's worn glasses since she was four, so she feels vulnerable when she's swimming without them. She even has prescription goggles.

"Then stop being annoying," I say. This morning was peaceful until Olive admitted she'd borrowed my hairbrush yesterday and lost it. Don't ask me how you can lose a hairbrush on a boat that's the size of a peanut, but Olive has managed to lose two in the past three days—hers and mine. I had to use Mom's comb on my hair this morning, and it wasn't pretty.

Now that we're swimming, though, I think I'll let my hair do its own thing and be kind of curly for the day.

Last night we slept in a spot where the currents aren't too strong, so Mom and Dad agreed to stay anchored for a couple of hours to let me and Olive jump in. We spent a few minutes doing dives off the bow of the boat, and now we're closer to shore, practicing our Little Mermaid move. That's when you go underwater and then jump up as high as you can, breaking the surface and throwing your head back at the same time so it creates a cascade of water over your profile. You have to stick your chest out too. Olive can't do it really well with short hair, but I taught her the move anyway. It's a good one.

I'm perfecting my form when I hear a small motor coming around the bend. It's sputtering and hissing, and I feel my heart speed up a little.

James.

I haven't seen him for a couple of days, but I've been wanting to. I've been turning over the word *real* in my head and wondering what he'd think if he knew me, really. If he knew what happened with Ethan and Amanda. If he knew everything.

But now that he's heading toward me and Olive, I'm not sure what to say.

Olive, however, is never at a loss for words.

James turns off the choking engine and glides near. Olive swims over and hangs her arms on the side of the dinghy, pulling herself halfway out of the water.

"Hey!" she says.

"Hey!" says James, imitating her enthusiasm.

Then he waves at me. "Hi," I say.

"Nice moves, Ariel."

Ack! He saw us doing that silly trick. I have the urge to dive under the water and hide. But that would be extra weird.

"You know the Little Mermaid?" I ask sheepishly.

"Of course," he says. "I spent a lot of summers at my neighborhood pool. My friends and I all loved it when the girls did that move, because—" He stops talking and laughs a little. "Well, because girls look good when they do it."

He gives me a wide grin, and I can't help but smile back.

"I thought you made up that move, Clem," says Olive, looking over her shoulder at me.

I shrug. "I guess Disney made it up."

Olive turns back to James.

"Are you taking us exploring again?"

"Not today," he says. I feel a pang of disappointment.

"My dad just wants to know if we should bring anything tonight," he says. "For dinner."

"Dinner?" I ask.

"Yeah," he says. "You didn't know your parents invited us over?"

"No."

"Oh," says James, his grin fading a little. "I thought maybe you—"

"Not that I don't want you to come!" I interrupt. "I just didn't hear about it."

"Yeah," he says, his smile brightening again. "They radioed over to us. We're meeting you guys at the next marina."

"Cool," I say. And it is cool. Even though my parents are meddling a little, maybe they noticed that I've been happier these past couple of days. Maybe they imagine it's got something to do with James. Maybe they're right.

I look over at *The Possibility* and see Dad pretending to read. But the book has fallen beside him and his hat is over his face. Total nap.

"I'll go ask what you should bring!" says Olive. She paddles toward the swimming ladder.

There's a moment of silence as we watch her swim over to the boat's ladder and climb up into the cockpit. It makes me nervous.

"She really liked the spaghetti," I say, kind of lamely. I want to say something more, something meaningful, because I've been thinking a lot about James since I left the dock in Paducah. But nothing is coming to me.

"It's good," says James. "It was my mom's recipe. It *is* her recipe, I mean. I guess it'll always be her recipe."

"Oh," I say, not sure how to respond.

"Mom says just bring conversation!" shouts Olive from *The Possibility*.

"Roger that!" shouts James, smiling quickly and erasing the shadow that I know I saw cross his face.

He looks down at me. "See you tonight," he says. With that, he starts up the sputtering engine and heads back to *Dreaming of Sylvia*.

There are more tall ship tales this evening, and Mr. Townsend has my parents laughing embarrassingly hard again. But it's nice to have guests. Mom even made meatloaf from scratch. Dad helped a *lot*.

James looks at me a few times during dinner in a way that makes me think he wants to talk to me. You know, in that eyes-a-little-wider-than-usual, head-pointed-outside way? He isn't very subtle, actually, but I guess it's up to me to make it happen.

When Olive excuses herself to use the head, I create an opening.

"I'm going outside for some fresh air," I say, grabbing my extra-big UNC sweatshirt from the couch. It sounds like what people say in movies or something, and it works.

James follows. We walk out to the cockpit and then along the edge of the boat to the bow, where it will take longer for Olive to find us, and we'll hear her coming. I sit on top of the hatch over my parents' bedroom so she can't pop up that way.

"Did you—" I start.

And at the same time, James says, "I want to—"

"You go," I say, laughing.

"I have to tell you something," he says.

I nod. He looks serious.

"It's kind of sad," he says. "But don't stop me until I'm finished."

"Okay," I say solemnly.

"Last summer, after this trip, my mom and dad got separated," says James.

My eyes widen in surprise, but I stay quiet.

"My family's been doing this summer sailing trip for four years now, so it's kinda weird without her."

"Oh," I say quietly, thinking of Mr. Townsend and that day I saw him get emotional out on the water. "Yeah, that must be . . . weird."

I'm frustrated by how obvious I sound. I just don't know what to say.

But James doesn't seem to notice.

"It's been sort of okay—I've been trying not to think about it. She moved out and stuff, but I guess I thought . . ." He pauses. "Well, right before we left to go sailing, my dad got papers from her filing for an official divorce."

"Oh." Again, my eloquence is unparalleled.

"Yeah, it hit him kind of hard. I mean, me, too, but I knew when she moved out that it was probably . . . I don't know, the end or something. Anyway, I know I acted funny when you asked about her the other day, and I'm sorry I didn't explain that sooner."

"James, you don't have to—" I start, but he puts a finger up to my lips.

"S'mores!" shouts Olive from the cockpit. I turn to look at her and she sees my serious face. It quiets her, but it also makes her curious. She starts climbing toward us on the bow.

"Olive, not now." My voice is stern.

"It's okay," says James, softly to me. Then louder: "Crazy Olive, I love s'mores!"

Olive smiles tentatively. "Mom's using dark chocolate." She knows that's my favorite.

"Okay," I say. I hold my hand out to stop her from coming out to the bow. "Go back down and we'll meet you in the cockpit really soon."

She pauses for a minute, and then I guess she realizes I'm being serious and not just shutting her out of something because I'm annoyed with her. She slinks down to the cockpit.

James puts his arm around me and squeezes.

"Hey, Clem," he says. "I didn't mean to make you uncomfortable. I'm okay."

I nod and pull my sweatshirt sleeve over my hand.

"My dad, though," James continues. "He really doesn't like to talk about it. So can you maybe not mention this?"

I nod again, and suddenly I remember that Mom thinks James's mother is just off volunteering in Africa or South America or something. Maybe she got that wrong?

I shake my head and exhale loudly to clear my mind. I want to go back and make s'mores with a cheerful face, especially if Mr. Townsend gets upset around this topic.

Everyone is settled into the cockpit already, having after-dinner coffees. James and I sit near Olive and open a box of graham crackers. We have a little kitchen blowtorch—it's not quite traditional s'more-making, but it's fun to do out on the water. We even own four metal sticks that we use specifically for this purpose.

"Whoa, Crazy Olive!" says James as Olive goes first and lights her marshmallow on fire, totally scorching it.

"I like it when the outside gets all black," she tells him, arranging a square of chocolate on her cracker and topping it with the poor marshmallow and another cracker. When she bites into her s'more, she gets melty goo on the sides of her mouth.

"Hey, Crazy Olive, you've got a little . . ." James points at the edge of his mouth, but Olive just stares at him, smiling and content with her dessert, not appreciating what he's telling her.

"Wipe your mouth, Livy," I say, reaching below deck and grabbing a tissue. I'm still processing what James told me. Why is their boat still named *Dreaming of Sylvia* if James's parents are divorced? I'm trying to act normal, but I'm staring at my mom, who's talking animatedly with Mr. Townsend about the moon cycles. She is so far from her law office right now.

"Clem, how do you like yours?" James asks me.

"Huh?" I ask, tuning in to him slowly.

"Your marshmallows?" he asks.

"Oh, golden brown," I say. My voice comes out soft and quiet. James seems as cheerful as ever.

"May I?" he asks, spiking a marshmallow on his metal stick.

"Sure," I say.

He approaches the flame cautiously, turning the marshmallow at a slow and steady speed, making sure each corner gets heat and rolling the stick in his hand. After a minute, he pulls the stick from the fire and blows lightly on the marshmallow.

"Is it right?" he asks.

"It's perfect," I say, impressed by the even tone he got.

"Here," he says, putting it down on my waiting cracker-with-chocolate.

He makes one for himself, too, and I wait to eat mine until he's done. Then we crunch in together.

"Hey!" says Olive. "You have chocolate on *your* faces now!"

She sits back with her arms folded across her chest, satisfied that we've gotten what we deserve after calling her out.

James and I look at each other and start to laugh. I hand him a tissue and take one myself, but I don't feel self-conscious, and the sadness of what he told me about his mom being gone is fading. He's here, in the moment, and he's okay. So I can be okay too.

Just before James and his dad step off the boat to leave a little later, he pulls me aside with a touch on the small of my back.

Mr. Townsend is telling Mom and Dad what a good time he had. Olive is licking her fingers from her fourth s'more.

James whispers in my ear, "Come swimming with me tomorrow?"

I turn to face him, my mouth just inches from his, and I say, "Yes."

chapter thirty

"Want to see George Washington?" asks James.

"Uh . . . I'm not sure," I say. Everything he's said to me today has been a lead-up to a joke, so I'm smiling but wary.

"Sure you do," he says, and then he dunks his head underwater and pops up backward with all his hair in front of his face. He folds it over onto his head so it looks like a crazy old wig like they used to wear in, well, George Washington times.

"That's a new one for me," I say. "But can you do five flips in a row?"

I spring into action and start my underwater flips, knowing I can hold my breath for five, sometimes six, and feeling the water swirl all around me as I speed through the movements.

I emerge into the air and breathe in deeply. I spin around to find James, and he flashes a giant smile.

Then, without a word, he takes off underwater. I count seven rotations.

"Show off," I say when he emerges with a cocky grin.

"Always," he says, water dripping down his face. I smile back, and suddenly he puts a hand on my waist, pulling me closer to him.

"Clem?" he says.

"Yes?" I feel every nerve in my body stand on end. His hand is touching my bare torso. We're in the water, wet, and practically naked.

"Thanks for hanging out this summer," he says. "I'd be so bored without you." He pauses, and I think for a minute that he might lean in. But he adds, "And Crazy Olive, of course!"

Then he pushes me away and yells, "Race to the shore!"

He takes off like a bullet, and I'm left still feeling my heart beating in my stomach. But I snap out of that quickly and jump into action. I can at least avoid humiliating myself by keeping up.

He beats me by a few seconds, and we end up lying on the muddy shore, panting for breath. I feel the sun warm my wet skin, and I look up at the blue sky, listening to James's laugh, his utter joy. We haven't talked about his mom at all today.

"How do you do it?" I ask.

"Do what?" He sits up on one elbow and turns toward me.

"How do you act so happy?"

"I am happy," he says.

"But, I mean, how do you . . . ," I start, but I'm not sure how to ask him. "Don't you feel sad about the divorce and everything? Don't you miss your mom?"

He sits up all the way now, looking out at the water.

"Yeah, I think about her," he says, slowly, carefully. And when he says it, his hand moves toward his heart. It seems involuntary, sad, sweet. But then he moves his hand to the ground and digs into the mud a little bit. "It was her choice to leave, though."

"Yeah," I say. "I guess so." I sit up and look in his eyes to see if I'm upsetting him.

He grimaces. "Oh man, I'm not going to be that 'sad child of divorce' to you now, am I?"

I smile at him. "No way," I say.

"Good. Then maybe we can discuss how today is, like, the best day ever." He turns to the lake and opens his arms to the sky. "Look at that sun, look at the water, look at you."

When he faces me again, I feel my heart speed up.

James leans in, and when his lips touch mine, they're still a little bit wet, and we hold the softest, most perfect kiss for a few beats. I want to enjoy the moment, but I'm already narrating what I'm going to write in my journal later: *Best. Kiss. Ever.*

⛵

I devote a whole page to the kiss. I cannot include enough adjectives to get this feeling down. It involves fireworks, shooting stars, and sparklers on the dock, and it doesn't even feel like an exaggeration. Then, I write:

> James is having such a hard summer, and he still laughs. He still makes everyone around him feel happy and important. My problems with Ethan and Amanda seem tiny next to his. It's not like having your mom leave or something. Why can't I figure out how to deal with things like James does?

chapter thirty-one

I have trouble sleeping because I'm still feeling buzzy about the kiss. It's an almost-perfect feeling, like there are thousands of tiny happy bubbles inside me, making me warm and fizzy. But there's something missing: sharing it with Amanda.

Being Amanda's best friend was my favorite thing. Sometimes people would mix us up because we were always together, so when they'd talk about us, they'd say our names really quickly and end up with something like "ClemandAmanda." Eventually, we became "Clemanda." It had to happen.

There was this one Saturday last year when Amanda and I went for coffee. Or, I should say, we went for coffee dessert drinks, because we both have a sweet tooth and cannot steer clear of seasonal, foamy, flavored steaming beverages. We sat down at the table in the window of the café in the strip mall near my house and watched people pull in and out of the parking lot. It was probably March or April. I know it was rainy, because Amanda was wearing her light blue trench coat and yellow rain boots. She always knew how to be the cutest girl in the room, in a good way.

I had on black rubber Hunter boots, which I'd heard were cool somewhere. I still thought Amanda's yellow ones were the best—they had little sunshines on them.

And on that day, we didn't talk about Ethan.

"The book I'm reading has such a scary cover that I have to turn it backside-up before I go to sleep," said Amanda as we grabbed a table by the window.

I blew on the top of my steaming cinnamon latte. "I did that with an R.L. Stine book once. The demon cover was taunting me."

"Terrifying." Amanda shivers and smiles. "Oh, wait, did you see Paul Kantor's epic status updates last night?"

"He always has a steady stream of hilarious things to say—he's even funnier online than he is in real life. It's like, go become a professional comedian already."

"I know! My updates are so blah."

"No they're not!" I said.

"Nice of you to say, but when everyone who comments on your updates says something better than your actual update, you know you're just not that good at one-liners."

"I hate that!" I almost knocked over Amanda's mocha cappuccino with my hand. I get really animated sometimes. "It's so much pressure if someone's comment is smarter and funnier than your actual update!"

"Especially when you spent, like, twenty minutes crafting the update to be really good," she said.

"Yeah," I said. "And are you supposed to respond? Who can keep up that level of wit?"

"Paul Kantor," we said simultaneously, before erupting into laughter.

"Well, I love your updates," said Amanda.

"Thank you." I smiled at her. "Ditto."

"Speaking of updates, I talked to Grandma Rose yesterday," said Amanda. Grandma Rose is her ninety-two-year-old grandmother who used to take us to the movies and make us leave halfway through because it was "too darn loud!" Nevermind that she's nearly deaf. She's a sweet lady, though—she always bought us ice cream afterward.

"How is G-Rose?" I asked.

"I think she's okay," said Amanda. "I'd rather just go visit her, though. You know how it's hard to talk to older relatives on the phone?"

"Oh yeah," I said. "They can't hear you, and they get confused about who you are and stuff?"

"Exactly. So I'm shouting, 'It's AMANDA! Your GRAND-DAUGHTER!' And that's basically the whole conversation. Forget any sort of interesting exchange."

I laughed into my foam.

"Yeah, visits are better," I agreed. "But still, the phone calls probably mean a lot, even if they do kind of suck."

"Definitely," said Amanda. "I will always, always talk to Grandma Rose when Mom calls her."

"Of course!" I said. "Because one day you'll *be* Grandma Rose, and who wants to be old and alone with bratty grandkids who won't even call you?"

"Not me!" declared Amanda. "The karmic value of those calls alone is worth it."

When Amanda finished her last sip of latte, I snapped a phone photo of her with a foam mustache. It turned out supercute, so I showed her the screen.

"Isn't it extra special that I look especially good in candid photos?" she asked through the foam, giving me a sideways smile.

"Totally extra special," I said, taking our cups to throw them away by the door.

"We are awesome," she said, standing up and joining me at the exit. And even though we were being mock conceited and ridiculous, it was just in the company of each other, when we could do things like that.

Then we opened the double glass doors simultaneously and linked arms. We jumped through puddles all the way home, just because we wanted to. It was stormy and gray, but Amanda said, "Ooh! I bet there'll be a rainbow later."

And that's how being with Amanda made me feel, once upon a time.

chapter thirty-two

At the next marina, I'm perched on the bow of the boat with the binoculars. I'm pretending to look at birds across the river, but honestly? I'm scouting for *Dreaming of Sylvia*. I can feel sweat beading on my forehead as I sit out in the sun—it's intensely hot today. I pat my face with a towel and look through the binoculars again. James told me they'd definitely be here when we arrived, but there's no sign of them yet.

I've been thinking a lot about James. About his mom just up and leaving, about his father's hidden pain, about how he doesn't have a big support system—just his dad—to help him if he's feeling sad. About the kiss.

I can't stop replaying it in my mind. I even have an on-the-go playlist dedicated to it now. It includes the Elliott Smith song, of course—and I pictured my day swimming with James while I listened to it before bed last night.

But then I started to worry.

What if James finds out what I did with Ethan and decides that I'm a bad person? What if he thinks I'm a liar and a cheater and an awful friend? What if he never knows Amanda? What if he doesn't understand what I'm starting to realize: I don't miss Ethan, I miss *her*. James doesn't know me like my family does—he could easily just turn his back on me when he finds out.

What if he never kisses me again?

I have to tell him.

So when I finally do see *Dreaming of Sylvia* coming around the bend, I feel a mix of excitement and terror.

I go back into the cabin and put on more sunscreen, staring at my face in the mirror and steeling myself for what I need to do. James was strong enough to tell me about his mom. He trusted me that much. He deserves to know.

I peek around the corner, and I can hear that Olive is in the nav station with my dad. He's explaining the next leg of the trip to her. Her patience for nautical charts is inexplicable.

Outside in the cockpit, Mom is reading a detective novel. I hurry past her.

"I'm going to go say hi to James!" I say, edging toward the dock.

Mom smiles with pursed lips, like she thinks I'm up to something scandalous. That look is so embarrassing.

"What?" I ask.

"Nothing," she says, looking back at her book. "Have fun!"

I scowl for a second, but then I look back at her and feel a surge of affection. I'm so lucky to have my mom. I walk over and give her a quick kiss on the cheek. Before she can ask, "What was that for?" I'm hopping off the boat in hopes of getting ahead of my sister's "wait for me!" cries.

I reach the other end of the pier just as Mr. Townsend pulls *Dreaming of Sylvia* into the slip. James smiles and throws me a rope.

"Tie us up, Clem!" he shouts.

I show off my cleat knot, which takes about three seconds.

"That's a beaut!" says Mr. Townsend.

"Thanks," I say.

He goes around the other side to drop the dinghy in the water.

James jumps off the boat and onto the dock, then heads right for me, arms outstretched. It's a hug. Like, a boyfriend hug. A big haven't-seen-you-in-a-couple-of-days boyfriend hug. I think. *I hope this doesn't go away.*

"Want to swim?" asks James, pulling away from me and peeling off his shirt.

"Sure!" I'm already ahead of him, slipping my cotton dress over my head to reveal the floral bikini that has just the right amount of ruffle (which is "very little, but enough to flatter your butt," according to Amanda).

We jump off the dock to cool down and paddle around for a minute before I hear a third splash.

"Clem!"

Olive.

"Crazy Olive!" shouts James, swimming over to my little sister. He dunks his head underwater and then shows her the George Washington trick, which she finds hysterical.

This is not how I wanted today to go.

"Olive, can you swim to our boat and see if there's more sunscreen for me?" I ask. "I need to reapply."

"I just got here," she says.

"Please?" I ask sweetly.

She nods okay and starts breaststroking back to *The Possibility.* I feel guilty. But I have a plan, and I need to do this now before I chicken out.

"Hey, want to take me for a spin in the dinghy?" I ask James, already hoisting myself up over the side of the *Little James*. I do an incredibly clumsy leg-split-flop into the boat, and then I look down at James with a goofy grin.

He's trying not to laugh.

"It's okay," I say. "Even I know that move was ridiculous."

He bursts. It's not just a laugh, it's a *guffaw*. Then I start to laugh, too, and I sit upright, adjusting my bathing suit to be sure everything's covered.

James climbs in beside me and starts up the engine just as I see Olive get to the top of the swim ladder of *The Possibility*. She looks over at us.

"Wait!" she says, starting down the ladder again. "I'm coming!"

I look at James. He shrugs like it's fine with him. But it's not okay with me. I need a break from my little sister. I pretend I didn't hear Olive.

"See you in a little bit!" I shout. "Tell Mom we'll be back in an hour!"

I don't look to see her face fall, I just tell James to gun it, and he does. The engine sputters and we cruise out of the cove and around the corner. I don't look back, because I'm sure Olive is waving like mad to try to flag us down and come with us. James stares straight ahead too.

⛵

"Remember when you asked me what happened?" I say to James after he turns off the loud engine and we idle on the water for a minute. I have to jump into this or I'll avoid it forever. No small talk, no beating around the bush, just straight-up telling.

"Yeah," he says.

"I fell for my best friend's boyfriend," I say. It's just seven words, and it sounds so innocuous and so terrible all at once when I hear it out loud.

"Did you hook up with him?" he asks.

I can't read his eyes—I can't tell whether they're judging or curious or surprised, or something else entirely.

"No. I mean, not exactly." I look down at my hands, which are twisting in my lap. "I really liked him, and he really liked me. We kept spending time together, and . . . it was just really not okay."

It would almost be easier to explain if we *had* hooked up, because then there's this thing—this tangible thing—that was wrong. But as it is, I just have this bad feeling, and a whole lot of guilt.

James isn't looking at me anymore. He's frowning and staring at the water.

His silence makes me nervous, so I start to ramble. I try to express how it was with Amanda, how close we were. And then I tell him how Ethan and I just clicked in this way that made it seem like we were supposed to be together. But that I realize now that it's about Amanda, and I've lost her. And it's my fault. My heart starts pounding a little when I explain things—it sounds so dumb in parts, and so awful in others—but James just sits quietly, listening.

"I'm not sure what to say, Clem," he says when I'm finished. His eyes are still cast downward.

I feel a surge of regret for having rambled on so openly. Maybe I was wrong about James and this new thing we have. Maybe now that he knows this about me he won't want to hang out anymore. I can't blame him if he thinks I'm a bad person, but I can't stand the thought of the rest of the summer without him.

"Do you think I'm horrible?" I finally ask.

He doesn't answer, but when he looks up at me, his eyes are squinted in disapproval.

"We should go back," he says. He starts up the engine before I have a chance to stop him.

I feel my bottom lip start to quiver as the wind hits my face, and I lower my sunglasses and point my head up toward the sun—somehow that helps me avoid crying. When we get to the marina, I jump out into the water and swim to the dock ladder, climb it, and walk hurriedly to *The Possibility*.

I hate the look I saw on James's face. It's the same look I saw all over school the week after my drive with Ethan. It's the same look Amanda gave me. And I know exactly what it means: whatever we had going on, whatever James felt for me, is over.

In my rush to get away from him, I trip over something on the dock and land on one knee with my hands out in front of me.

"Ouch!" Great. There's definitely a huge splinter in my left palm.

I raise my sunglasses and look around to see what caused my fall. Mrs. Ficklewhiskers is behind me, giving me the eye. Is it me, or does she look amused?

"Clem, dear, are you all right?" Ruth is pushing herself up out of her folding chair.

I put up my hand. "Don't get up, Ruth—it's okay." I stand and inspect my palm. The splinter is too small for me to grab with my fingers. How can something so tiny pack such big pain?

"George, get the kit!" shouts Ruth, who has appeared at my side. "That wily old cat!"

She takes my hand gently and leads me to her chair. "Sit, dear. We'll fix you up in no time."

George sticks his head out of their cabin and steps out onto the dock with a green metal box in his hand.

"I was a nurse in the Korean War." Ruth takes the case from George and opens it up.

"I bet you looked cute in your uniform," says George, looking at her affectionately.

"Oh, Georgie, stop!" says Ruth, giggling.

I smile in spite of myself.

"It's not bad," I say. "Just a splinter."

"Let Ruthie take it out," says George. "Those things can get infected."

Ruth grabs the tweezers from her kit and focuses in on the sliver of wood poking out from my palm. Her hand wavers a little bit at first, but it steadies as she grabs the splinter and pulls it out cleanly.

"You'll live." She winks at me.

"I don't know," says George, helping me to my feet. "I think she may need some extra medicine. James! Get over here!"

I freeze.

"Come on!" George shouts, waving his arm in the direction of James's boat. "Your girl needs a kiss."

Obviously James is refusing to come over and help me because he hates me and thinks I'm a monster, which I am, so who can blame him? I will myself not to look.

"Oh, honey, what is it?" asks Ruth softly.

That's when I realize that the tears I've been holding onto since James first looked at me all squinty on the dinghy have started to leak out. I put my hand on my cheek and it's wet. *Ack.*

"Nothing," I say, quickly wiping my face with the back of my hand.

George gives up on James and kneels down next to my chair.

"Did you have a fight?" he asks.

How did I end up here, on a dock in the middle of nowhere, with two old people saving me from splinters and asking about my love life?

I nod and sniffle. There's no point in hiding it now that I'm openly crying.

"Fights come from relationships with great passion in them," says Ruth.

"That's right," George agrees. "You don't get mad at people you don't care about."

"Georgie and I have had some doozies." Ruth puts her hand to her forehead like she can't even bear to *think* of how bad their fights have been.

I smile meekly. "Thanks . . . I'm sure it'll be okay."

"You don't sound sure," says George. "Want to talk about it?"

I shake my head no. Then I stand up quickly, realizing that I'm keeping a seat from the two practically elderly people who are kneeling near me. Something is wrong with this picture.

"I have to—" I start. But then I remember that I don't really have to do anything. I just want to get out of the sun, back to my tiny cabin, where I should have stayed all summer, listening to sad music and punishing myself rather than venturing out and hoping against hope that someone would see past the fact that I'm a lying, cheating, horrible person.

Ruth looks at me with sympathy in her eyes. "Whatever he did, he's a good kid," she says. "We know James."

I nod again. *But he didn't do anything*, I think. *It's me you don't know.*

"It was my fault," I say.

"Nonsense!" George shakes his head. "You're too sweet to be at fault."

I raise my eyebrows at him. "That's what you think," I say.

"What could you have possibly done?" asks Ruth. "We know you didn't run around on him—the only other boaters out here have one foot in the Senior Center."

I shrug and turn to go. They wouldn't understand.

"James had a hard year," says Ruth, grabbing my arm. "I don't know if he told you why his mom—"

George puts his hand up. "Now, Ruth," he says, "that's not ours to share."

Ruth purses her lips but doesn't finish her thought. She smiles warmly at me. "Whatever you fought about, he'll come around."

"Thanks." I take a step back toward *The Possibility*. "I hope so."

chapter thirty-three

When I come out of my room later for dinner, I've decided something. I need to tell my family what happened too. Not, like, exactly—but I want them to know. I want it to be out in the open, even if it means them looking at me like James did today.

So when Mom asks if there was something that upset me today, instead of saying no or shrugging it off, I just tell them.

"I told James about the whole thing with Amanda from last year," I say. "And he pretty much defriended me. Just like Amanda did on Facebook. But she didn't defriend Ethan."

I'm not sure they'll even know what I mean, but I can tell instantly that they want to try.

"Clem, what is it that really happened last year?" asks Dad.

I look up at him. His eyes are teacher eyes, the ones he gets around a student who's in trouble. They're understanding, but they're also my father's. How can I tell my father what I did? Do I even *get* what I did?

I look at Mom. She nods, the same question on her face.

Olive is staring down at her hot dog and beans.

"I sort of fell for Amanda's boyfriend," I say. "We just kept getting closer and closer."

I tell them about the online chatting, the time we went to the movies, how we'd exchange glances at lunch and in history class. Dad even laughed when I told them about the *Simpsons* Civil War joke. He got it.

It was nice to tell them; it didn't feel terrible like I thought it would. We all ate slowly while I talked, and I could picture us with our hot dogs, mustard at the corners of our lips. It felt okay, but when I got up to the part about the drive we took, my mind was racing with what to say.

"The day I got my license, Ethan and I went for a drive," I say. "We ended up talking a lot, and almost . . ."

"Hooking up?" asks Dad.

"Not 'hooking up,'" I say, embarrassed that Dad even used that term. It's so weird to be telling your dad this. I don't think if we were back home in Bishop Heights that I could ever tell him. "We didn't do anything at all, except hold hands a little. But it felt like . . ."

"You felt like his girlfriend," says Olive. I look down at her and see that she's totally caught up in this story, my story, and she's understood me perfectly. I want to hug her.

"Yeah. And when we got back to town and saw Amanda, she knew." I drop my head and look at the table. All of our plates are empty, but no one has moved to pick them up. "She just knew," I say again, quietly.

"What was it that she knew?" asks Mom.

"That we liked each other, I guess." I don't even know how to define it. "That we maybe wanted more."

"So Amanda broke up with him?" asks Olive.

I shake my head no.

"I've seen this a lot," says Mom, frowning. "The man gets forgiven while the woman wears a scarlet letter."

Mom's a lawyer, but she was an English major in college. She deals with tragedy through literature. It's only sometimes helpful. Luckily, I've read that one.

"Call me Hester Prynne," I say.

"Hester who?" asks Olive.

"She's the main character in *The Scarlet Letter*, Livy," says Dad. "She has an affair while she's married and becomes an outcast."

"But Clem's not married," says Olive.

"It's not a perfect metaphor," says Mom.

"Forget it, Olive," I say. I glance down at the bun crumbs on my plate and wonder how to feel. What to do.

"I'm worried about next year," I say. "I don't really . . ." I pause for a minute. "I don't really have any friends."

A tear slips down my cheek, and the room is totally silent for a moment.

Then Dad clears his throat. "Clem, I know it looks very dark right now. But you don't have to dwell on this. The heart wanders—it's part of being young. You know who you are, and we know who you are."

"I'm not sure I know who I am," I say. Because it's true. How can I have any idea who I am? All I have to go on are my past actions, and this thing that I did last year, it was terrible, even though it's so hard to put my finger on.

"Want me to tell you?" asks Olive.

I look up at her, and I guess something in my eyes says yes, so she goes ahead.

"You are the big sister who braids me," she says. I glance at her near dreads.

"I'm about to become the big sister who forcibly washes your hair," I say.

She reaches up and touches her matted curls protectively.

"You can drive stick exceptionally well," says Dad.

"You think so?" I ask.

"Without question," he says.

"You love to read in the sun, just for fun," says Mom.

I smile at her, though I'm about to get cheesy chills from the self-help session I feel starting up.

"You can tie the perfect knot for any given situation," says Olive.

"You record your life in that journal," says Mom. "You may write a book one day, if you want to."

I raise my eyebrows. Mom the English major doesn't give that kind of compliment lightly.

"You do the best Little Mermaid jumps," says Olive.

"You listen to music that really means something to you," says Dad.

I feel my stomach unclench a little bit. I let my shoulders relax. I think about the song that James gave me, "Clementine." I take a deep breath.

"Are we making you cry yet?" asks Olive. Then she starts to giggle, and I reach over and squeeze her tight.

chapter thirty-four

Two days later, I'm hanging on to my family's kind words, forgiving myself a little more. It feels good, but I can't deny that James is on my mind too. We docked at the next marina, and James and his dad were due in yesterday, but *Dreaming of Sylvia* never showed up. Now we're about to leave again. What if James isn't going to forgive me? What if I don't see him again? There's only one week left of summer.

Okay, I'm more than getting worried. I'm full-blown panicking.

The only way I can get in touch with James is by radio, and I haven't gotten up the nerve to ask Mom and Dad if I can call him on the official Tombigbee Waterway frequency. Besides, it's not like I can make it a private call. It'd be like calling a guy who may hate you on speakerphone, and he'd be on speakerphone too.

I keep imagining myself sounding totally needy.

"Uh, James, where are you?"

"Clem, I never want to talk to you again. I can't be with a girl who would hurt her best friend like that."

My mind is not a very forgiving place.

I look down at my hands—my fingernails are bitten down to nubs. I have to do something.

"Dad?" I ask, poking my head into the nav station while he fiddles with the gauges before we push off.

"Yes?" asks Dad, not looking up from his panel.

I glance at the radio. "Never mind," I say, my insecurities bubbling up again.

"Clem!" Olive grabs my hand as I slink out of the nav station. "Let's walk outside. The sun is setting, and Mom says we can see it sink into the water from the other side of the dock."

Watching the sun set into a river is one of the best things in the world. One day I want to go all the way to the west coast so I can see it happen over the real ocean, but for now, smaller bodies of water will do.

I nod at my sister and follow her off the boat, grabbing two folding deck chairs from the under-bench storage area.

Down a few slips on the dock, we spot Ruth and George sitting with matching silver sun catchers under their chins.

"You guys should use sunblock!" says Olive, folding her hands across her chest. She always has the rudeness—or is it courage?—to say what I don't.

Ruth smiles at us, not bothered.

"Honey, we're old," she says to Olive. "Something else'll get us before skin cancer does!"

I can tell that Olive is about to object, but then she gets distracted.

"Hey," she says. "Did you change your boat's name?"

I look to where she's gesturing and see the words *True Love* in elaborate script on the hull. Faintly underneath it, now that Olive has pointed it out, I can see that the boat used to be called something else. That isn't unusual—people buy used boats and rename them all the time—but I see George look sideways at Ruth. She gives him a small smile and nods.

"We did indeed," says George. "She used to be called *Linda*."

I raise my eyebrows, and Ruth giggles. She looks my age for a second.

"Georgie's old girlfriend," says Ruth.

"Girlfriend?" says George, mock indignantly. "She was my wife for thirty years!"

"Until I came along," says Ruth.

"That's right, honey," says George, leaning over to take her hand. "Ruthie and I—we were meant to be."

"*True Love*," says Ruth, pointing to the boat's name.

Olive grins.

I want to ask if Linda died, or if they got divorced, or if Ruth and George had an affair. I guess George sees the questions on my face, because he says, "Linda lives in Boca Raton now. I hear she has a new boyfriend."

"Oh." It's all I can think of to say.

Olive and I wave at them and keep walking to the edge of the dock, where we set up our chairs to watch the sunset.

"That was funny," she says, adjusting her legs so they don't get pinched by the plastic seat.

"What?"

"How George left Linda for Ruth." Her voice rises excitedly.

I lean back in my chair, not saying anything.

"Do you think he was married when they met?" Olive asks.

I shrug. I'm curious, but I'm not sure I want to talk about this.

"Well, do you think Linda hates Ruth? That they had a big falling-out and he blew her in the dust?"

I laugh at my sister. "I think you mean left her in the dust, or blew her off," I say. "Why didn't you ask *them* if you're so curious, Livy?"

She sits back in her seat. "Maybe I will."

We watch the sun get lower and lower in the sky. The last minutes of a sunset go by in a heartbeat. One moment the sky is brilliant gold, and the next, blue darkness descends, with just a hint of rosy glow to show you where the sun once was.

The reflection of that pink shimmer is still shining on the water when Olive says, "I guess I don't think it matters—they're so happy together."

I look over at her, and she's looking up at me for confirmation.

"You're right, Livy," I say. "If 'true love' and 'meant to be' are clichés to be used, Ruth and George are the people you'd use them about."

When we get back to the boat, I make a call on the radio. I think we get through to *Dreaming of Sylvia*, but I can't be sure. There's a lot of static, and I can't tell if it's James or his dad who answers. You're not really supposed to ramble on the radio—it's for quick communication. So here's what I say: "James, it's Clem. I'm what's real."

The next morning, there's a soft knock at my door. I've been awake and had my iPod on for an hour or so, but I'm not brooding. I made a new playlist, one that even has some upbeat songs on it. I've been writing in my journal, too, in colored pencil. I'm sick of black ink.

"Come in, Livy," I say.

But it's not Olive.

"Oh," I say, sitting up on my bed and closing my journal quickly.

"Your mom let me in," says James. He runs his hand through his hair and then rests it in his shorts pocket.

"Can I . . . ?" he asks, gesturing toward the bed.

"Sure."

He closes the door behind him and sits down next to me on the bed. That would be weird in a normal room, but this cabin is pretty much door, bed, drawers, and one foot of floor space, so it's okay. Besides, I want him this close.

He's got a mint in his mouth. I can see him working it around his cheek, and he smells good, like morning sunshine and soap and peppermint.

"I'm sorry I freaked out the other day," he says. "It's just—"

He doesn't finish his thought, and after a long moment of silence, I say, "I know it was probably shocking to hear that I did that."

He smiles at me sideways. "Seeing as how I thought you were perfect and all, right?"

I half grin back. "Right."

And it's funny, because I still feel as bold as I felt last night making that radio call. I know James maybe came to tell me he can't be with me, that he isn't up for dealing with someone who could betray a friend like I did, or that he could never trust me after what I confessed. But I'm not afraid, no matter what he's here to say.

James looks down at his lap. "So there's more to the story about my mom leaving."

"Okay," I say.

"She kind of left with this other guy," he says. "Our neighbor, actually."

"Oh." *Oh.*

"So I have this weird thing with, like, cheating," he says.

I bite my lip. "Most people have a weird thing about cheating," I say. "That's why it's called cheating."

"Yeah." James looks up at me. "But I realized that what happened with my mom doesn't really have much to do with you."

"Thanks," I say.

"I mean, what you did was *not* cool."

"I know." I rush in to defend myself. "I just wanted—"

James puts a finger to my lips. "Let me finish."

I look up at him hopefully.

"I mean, you should *not* have let it go on for so long," he says, not fully letting me off the hook. "But it happens."

"It does?" I ask.

"On TV, way worse stuff happens every week," he says. "If your life is like a CW drama, you and your friends should be back on track by 10 p.m."

I smile again. "Thanks for listening."

"Thanks for telling me." He laughs a little bit. "Also, thanks for calling yourself a heel—that was classic."

"Huh?"

"On the radio," he says. "Isn't that what you said? 'I'm a heel.'"

"No!" I shake my head. "I said 'I'm what's *real*,' you dork! Like what you said to me when you gave me the drawing."

James's mouth opens wide into a huge laugh. It takes him a minute to recover before he says, "That is so cheesy!"

I swat him on the leg. "You thought I called myself a *heel*? Who even says that?"

"I don't know," he says, still smiling. "I thought it was hilarious, though. I thought you were trying to make me laugh to get me out of my own judgmental mindset."

"Oh," I say. "Well, I'm glad it worked."

"So I guess whatever happened with you and your friends last year doesn't have much to do with us."

I love that word: *us*. It's the best, most simple, most incredible two letters ever put together. He puts his hand out on the bed between us, palm open. I take it and twine my fingers through his.

And we're in my cabin with the door closed, remember? So next comes the kissing.

⚓

After a few minutes (okay, maybe an hour) of making up, James and I go above deck and spend a little while hanging out on the bow of *The Possibility* as the sun rises in the sky.

Amazingly, my family seems to have disappeared for the time being. I guess we're not leaving the marina today.

I snuggle up against James as he leans back on the open hatch.

"I have a game," he says.

"What kind?"

"Corny boat names," he says. "I'll start—*Nauti Girl*." He spells it out for me, and I laugh.

"Okay, I've actually seen *Knotty Buoy*." I say. "As in K-N and B-U-O-Y."

"No way—that's terrible!"

"I know."

"*Fox-Sea Lady*," he counters.

"*Surfvivor*," I say.

"*Knot Tonight*."

"*Frayed Knot*."

"I think I've seen that one!" His chest rises with laughter. "They dock in Chicago sometimes, right?"

"Yes!" I turn around to face him. "It took me forever to get the double meaning, and when I did, I thought, *Not worth the effort.*"

He laughs. "Okay, *Boatilicious.*"

I smirk at him. "Have you noticed that all of yours are a little naughty?"

"Are you spelling that K-N-O-T-T-Y?" he asks. "Because you should. You're a boat girl, you know."

I lean back against him again and laugh, and I imagine that comment would have made me bristle at the beginning of the summer. But now, being a boat girl seems like a pretty cool thing.

⛵

When he smiles at me, I feel like I'm sitting under a heat lamp. I live for the times when his fingers brush my leg at lunch, or when we pass in the hallways and he raises his eyebrows at me, like we have a secret. I should feel bad—and I do, most of the time—but how can I stop thinking about him when seeing his face makes me feel so alive?

I know you're not supposed to look back on your diary until you're, like, forty or something, but I often flip to a few months ago and reread what I wrote. It seems like my feelings change all the time, so even just a little while back I might have seen things totally differently.

Case in point: I can't believe I wrote that entry about Ethan just two months ago! The way I'm feeling now, about James, is so much better. It's like Ethan was just in my imagination somehow. Nothing was ever real with him. He was with Amanda. James is with me.

chapter thirty-five

"But you're *always* with him!" shouts Olive, sticking her lower lip out in a world-class pout.

"I am *not*," I say. "We're out *at sea* and we're not even on the same boat! I'm on a boat with *you*. How could I always be with him?"

My logic is flawless.

"Whenever we dock at a marina, you run over to *Dreaming of Sylvia* and you won't let me come with you," she says. "It isn't fair."

I look to Mom for help, but she just shrugs.

"Olive is making a valid request, Clem," she says. "She wants to spend time with you."

"You and James *have* been hanging out a lot," says Dad.

I roll my eyes.

"Not that there's anything wrong with that," says Mom. "You know we like James. I just think your little sister wants some attention too."

"She has all day with me almost every day!" I say. "We're trapped on a *boat*, in case you guys haven't noticed."

"Please, can I come with you today?" asks Olive.

How can I explain to my ten-year-old sister that what I really want to do is go over to James's boat and curl up with him in his cozy stateroom and kiss until my mind is completely scrambled? That's what I've been doing for the past week, whenever we're docked together, which James and I are making sure happens basically whenever we're docked.

We haven't discussed the Ethan and Amanda situation a lot, but I did tell him about the day I went on Facebook and saw that she and Ethan were back together.

"That's crazy," said James.

"I know," I said.

"You didn't have any messages from the guy, what's his name?" he asked.

"Ethan."

"Ethan," he said, like the sound of the name bothered him. "You didn't have any messages from him?"

"No."

"Does that make you upset?" he asked.

"Not really." I was more upset about the "BITCH" message from Amanda, but I didn't mention that—I didn't want to face it.

"Are you over him?" asked James.

"I think so," I said, truthfully. "But I mean, I don't know if I have anything to get over. It wasn't real."

He smiled, brushing back a piece of hair from my forehead. "You still felt something."

"Yeah," I said. "But I spent the beginning of the summer thinking that the pain I was in had to do with missing Ethan, like he was what mattered."

"He broke your heart, huh?" asked James.

"No," I said. "At first that's what I thought the hurt was about. But I don't think it was."

"What do you mean?"

"He didn't break my heart," I said. "I did. Losing Amanda did. It isn't about Ethan."

James looked at me then, and a smile started to spread across his face.

"Good," he said. "Because this Ethan kid? He sounds like a dick."

I let a little laugh escape me then, and James pulled me in for more kissing. I know they say laughter's the best medicine, but kissing? It's definitely also Top 5.

"Clem!" shouts Olive, shaking me out of my in-the-cabin-with-James dream state. "Please, *please* let me come today?"

I look at her pathetic pout. It's easier for me and James to, um, snuggle on his boat because his dad usually takes the dinghy out fishing as soon as they tie up at the marina. He got mad at us the other day when we hijacked it to go for a ride because we didn't get back until after six, and he "needs to have a line in by 4 p.m."

Lightbulb!

"Okay, Olive," I say. "You can come with me."

"Yay!" she says, rushing over and attacking my waist with a little-armed bear hug.

Then I say, real casually, "Oh, why don't you bring your fishing rod?"

"Do you guys fish off the boat?" asks Olive.

"Um, sometimes!" I say.

Mom eyes me suspiciously.

"We do," I lie. "I mean, we would if we felt like it."

Dad laughs. "Fishing? Is that what they call it these days?"

Could my parents be more humiliating?

"Let's go," I say to Olive. Then I stick my tongue out at Mom and Dad. They both laugh at me.

When we get to *Dreaming of Sylvia*, James greets us from the cockpit.

"Hey, hey, lovely ladies," he says.

Olive grins and takes James's hand as she boards the boat.

I step up on my own.

"Hi there," he says to me, kissing me quickly on the lips.

"Sorry about this," I whisper, eyeing Olive. "I was thinking maybe she and your dad might—"

"Dad's kind of sick today," interrupts James. "I was hoping we could go to your boat, actually."

"I'd rather not," I say, half smiling. Although I'm in a loving-my-parents phase, I do need some time away. The hours on *Dreaming of Sylvia* have saved me these past couple of weeks. And not just because of the kissing.

"Yeah!" says Olive. "That boat gets *booooring*."

James smiles. "Okay, we'll stay here. Let's set up on the dock, though. I don't want to wake up Dad."

He grabs three towels and we spread them out along the wooden planks near the boat. Olive drops a line in next to the pier, where she'll probably only catch little sunfish, if she hooks anything. But she's happy to be included.

And really? I don't mind having her here. If we're not going to kiss in the cabin anyway, that is.

"My mom used to fish off the dock," says James, once we get settled onto our towels. We're both leaning against a wooden pole, sitting side by side as Olive casts and reels, casts and reels, in front of us.

"Oh yeah?" asks Olive. "What did she catch?"

"She never caught much." He laughs and looks far away, like he's thinking back. "It didn't matter, though."

He turns to face me, and his eyes are lit up with remembering. "Dad would come back from fishing out on the dinghy like he still does, and Mom would send me into the cabin to wash up for dinner. Then she'd look in the cooler for Dad's biggest catch. When I came out of the cabin—and this went on until I was, like, ten—she'd hold up the biggest fish and pretend that she'd just caught it. Dad would beam at her like he was so proud, and she'd laugh and laugh. I thought she was a magical fisherman, always catching something when I wasn't looking."

I smile. "That's funny."

"She was a practical jokes person," he says. "She always had an entertaining way to trick me."

"You didn't go out fishing with your dad?" I ask.

"Nah," he says. "I usually stayed on the boat and hung out with Mom. Dad's fishing ritual is kind of solitary, actually."

"I love fishing with my dad," says Olive, reeling in another empty hook. She doesn't even frown, though, just casts it back out into the water with a flick of her wrist.

"Yeah," says James. "I loved dock fishing with Mom too. And I always believed it was her catch, somehow. Dad didn't even mind."

"Is it hard to, you know . . . remember stuff about her?" I ask. I'm thinking about Amanda, and how every time I've thought of her this summer, the memory has come with a sharp pang, because maybe it feels like she's gone, really gone.

"No," says James. "She's still my mom."

"Really?" I ask, surprised. "You're not, like, mad or something?"

"No," he says, shaking his head adamantly.

I tilt my head and look at him, wondering at the way he carries on, just smiling, so effortlessly. How does he do it?

He must see the question in my eyes, because then he says, "I was. Believe me, I was. I didn't talk to her for months—Dad made me go to therapy a few times and everything."

I look over at Olive, who's concentrating on her rod. "And that helped?" I ask.

"Yeah," says James. "It did. I wish my dad would go, though. I think it would help him realize that even though it ended, the memories of us as, like, a family are still there, almost tangible."

"What do you mean?"

"Just because the situation turned out kind of messed up doesn't mean that my memories aren't valid," he says. "They're still true, still real."

He shakes his head, laughing at himself. "I'm kind of quoting my therapist," he admits.

I lean back on the pole and smile. I want to play his words over and over so I'll remember them. When I first met James, I thought he rambled on and on, but none of the guys at my school are as eloquent as he is. Does it come with having a mom leave?

"Like, there was this time when my mom caught me trapping fireflies in a jar in our backyard," says James. "They were running out of air and I had no idea, so she shook them free. She promised that they'd come back that summer to light up for me in thanks, and that we could sit outside and talk to them, just like our whole backyard was a jar full of magic. She and I sat out there every night before Dad got home from work—just watching them and making up names for them and telling stories. I swore I could tell them apart, though I guess I was imagining that, because who can even tell a girl firefly from a boy firefly—let alone specific named fireflies. But it was the best . . ."

I watch Olive cast out again, jig her reel at a little nibble, and then sit quietly and wait for a bigger bite. The sunlight glints off of her glasses. The waves lap at the boats beside us. James's red hair blows softly in the summer breeze as he talks. He does ramble. But it's the best. I look around at him, at Olive, at the waves.

"Got it," I say, interrupting him.

"Got what?" asks James.

I smile and give him a light kiss. "My memory of today."

chapter thirty-six

You draw like a true artist.
You're nice to my little sister.
You have the best hair color on the planet.

I pause, chewing the end of my marker. We're sailing today—trying to reach the Mississippi border. It's the beginning of our last week out on the water. I can't believe the summer's almost over.

Olive knocks on my door.

"What are you doing?" she asks.

I hesitate, but then decide she can be helpful.

"I'm making a list for James," I say.

"Of what?"

"Just nice things about him," I say. I want it to be a list of things like the stuff my family said to me the other night, things maybe he doesn't hear. I feel bad about that—everyone should know the nice things about themselves.

"Are you going to give it to him?" she asks.

"Of course!" I say.

"So it's not like your diary or private or anything?" she asks.

"Nope," I say, glad I haven't gotten very far. I'm definitely going to add some kissing stuff after Olive leaves.

She sits down on my bed and tilts her head, thinking.

"He talks really fast when he's excited," she says.

I write it down, and then I add, "You talk slowly and thoughtfully too."

"He smiles and laughs all the time."

"You're right," I say, copying that onto the page.

"He makes *you* smile," she says.

I blush, but I write it down.

"I really like him, Clem," she says.

I almost write, "Olive really likes you," but then I realize she's just saying that to me. Like, approving of him for me.

"Thanks, Livy."

"He's not anyone's boyfriend, is he?" she asks, her eyes wide.

I laugh at her. That question probably would have sent me scowling earlier this summer, but now I know myself better, I know I'm not that girl.

"He's *my* boyfriend," I say.

"Good," she says, hopping off the bed. "I'm gonna go get a snack."

She runs out of the room and I go back to thinking about James. My *boyfriend*. I feel a giddy smile cross my face.

You joke around with Ruth and George and think that "old people rule."

Your kisses make me feel like I'm dancing.

You found me a new song with my name in it.

211

As we get closer to the next marina, I peek out the window and see James standing on the dock. There's a light rain falling, and his red hair is blowing all around his face. His hands are in his pockets, and he looks like he's been waiting.

"James!" I hear Mom greet him from the cockpit.

"Clem?"

James is calling my name.

I scramble up into the cockpit and lean over the side of the boat, out into the rain.

"Hey!" I shout, unable to squelch my grin. As soon as we're tied up, I jump off the boat and onto the dock.

James opens up his arms. I squeeze him tightly.

That's when I notice he's shaking a little.

I pull back. "What's wrong?"

"I need your help," he says. "I need ... I think I need your dad."

"What's going on?" I ask.

I feel Mom step down onto the dock—she must see that James isn't himself.

"James, what is it?" she asks.

He bites his lip then, and I have the urge to sweep him up in my arms and hold him close. But my mom is here. And she does it instead.

He leans on her shoulder and lets her hug him. I feel so helpless. I don't know what to do.

Olive peeks her head out from the cockpit and then disappears. A few seconds later, she and Dad are on the dock with us.

Mom lets James go, and he wipes his face with the back of his hand.

"I'm sorry," he says, looking at my dad. "I didn't know who to ask ..."

"What's wrong, son?" asks Dad, and I love him for his tone, for his Dad-ness.

"He just got so angry all of a sudden." James hangs his head like he's ashamed. "He's mad at her, I know, but this time it's . . ."

"Your father?" asks Dad.

James nods.

Olive and Mom stay behind, but Dad and I follow James to the other side of the marina, where *Dreaming of Sylvia* is docked.

Before we went, James had to explain to Mom and Dad about his mom. They looked a little shocked—Mr. Townsend hadn't even told them about the separation. That didn't surprise me after seeing him hide his tears that one day, but I didn't bring it up— that moment feels private and sacred, still.

When we reach the boat, James brings us around to the back. That's when I see the scratches on the aft end, where the cursive letters that spelled out *Dreaming of Sylvia* used to be.

"He used a screwdriver or something, I think," says James, running a hand over the angry marks.

Dad puts his arm on James's shoulder. "Let me talk to him."

We slowly climb aboard. James goes into the cabin first, followed by my dad. I hesitate for a moment, wondering if I should be here.

I take a deep breath, though, and I step inside too. It's stuffy in the living room, like no one's opened the windows for a day. Then I notice that there are books pulled off the shelf, and a broken glass lies on the floor. Dad and I wait in the main cabin while James knocks on the master V-berth door.

I stare at the photo I saw that first night we had dinner on *Dreaming of Sylvia*. The glass over it is shattered in a spiderweb pattern reaching from the center, but I can still make out the image. James looks about three or four, and his mom is holding him in her lap while his dad stands above them with his hand on her shoulder. She has his red hair. I feel a rush of sadness for their broken family and I think I might cry, but then I hear James opening the door to the V-berth.

I hear Mr. Townsend say something in a muffled tone, and James peeks his head back out.

"He doesn't really want—" starts James.

Dad moves forward.

"James," he says softly. "Let me. You and Clem go up top."

James nods and comes back into the main cabin. He looks at me and gives me a half grin. Always trying.

"Let's get some sun," he says quietly.

I go outside and we step our way up to the bow. We plop down on the hatch above the V-berth. James leans against the mast and I sit next to him, crossing my legs in front of me.

I realize that we can hear them. James's dad is shouting, calling James's mom a bunch of pretty awful things.

I look over at his face, but he doesn't seem embarrassed. He holds my gaze.

"He's so sad," James says softly, and my mind echoes back to when Olive said that about me, at the beginning of the summer. That seems so long ago. The problem I was dealing with seems very small right now.

"I know," I say. I put my hand over James's and he opens his palm to hold it.

I hear my dad talking quietly to Mr. Townsend.

"It's all right," he says. "It's going to be just fine. You're going to be okay."

He used to say that to me when I was little. He's talking to Mr. Townsend like you talk to a kid. I guess sometimes adults need that, too, because after a minute Mr. Townsend's yelling seems to quiet down.

Then I hear my dad's voice get a little louder, a little firmer.

I feel like I'm in a movie, like I'm watching a climactic scene, and I can picture my dad down there, talking to Mr. Townsend. My dad is the good guy, the wise hero. James and I are the kids, the audience, just watching. Mr. Townsend is the one who needs saving. There is no bad guy—not really.

"It will always be hard," says my dad. "But this is your time with James. Don't waste it. My time with Clem and Olive has been priceless this summer."

James squeezes my hand, and I look out at the water, still listening to my dad.

"The yelling, the laughing, the eye rolling, the dirty hair—everything," he says. "It's all part of the magic."

I feel a tear roll down my cheek. It gets quiet for a minute, and I look over at James again. He's smiling at me.

"You're so lucky," he says.

"I know."

⛵

James and I go for a walk around the docks, and by the time we get back to the boat, Dad has talked Mr. Townsend into taking a navy shower. He steps off the boat, hair still wet, and reaches out to give James a hug.

"I'm so sorry," says Mr. Townsend.

James just holds him tightly and whispers, "I love you, Dad."

What guy can say that? It makes me love *him*.

chapter thirty-seven

I press the pen into my journal and the words come fast and furious as I lean against the life jacket at the edge of the dinghy. When I got back to *The Possibility*, I grabbed my diary and the pink feather pen, untied the *Sea Ya*, climbed in, and floated away without asking.

Last summer, before Ethan moved to Bishop Heights, before there was even a wisp of a possibility that I'd spend a summer without Amanda's friendship, she and I had a different kind of fight.

"I'm definitely going to college in-state," said Amanda, her feet running up the wall of my bedroom next to the closet. She was flipping through the magazine Mom had left on my bed, the one that ranked all the colleges.

She'd slept over, and we were spending the morning just hanging out in my room, as usual. This type of nothing-to-do day was one reason we were both dying to get our drivers' licenses.

I was sitting at my desk trying to restring beads onto my favorite necklace, which was broken.

"Not me," I replied. "I'm going far away."

I said it without thinking; I was focused on the blue turquoise piece in front of me, trying to thread its hole with the gold chain that would barely fit through.

But Amanda dropped her legs to the floor and sat up to face me. "Where?" she asked.

I shrugged without looking up. "Just somewhere else," I said. "Somewhere less boring."

She stood up then, turning away from me and grabbing her bag. "I'm going to call my mom to get me," she said.

"Why?" I looked up for the first time.

"I just have to go."

That day, I thought she just got suddenly tired, or hot, or PMS-y. The next day she was back to smiles and fun. I'd almost forgotten about it completely.

But as I relive it with my pen, writing down what happened that morning, I'm doing what Henry does when he holds up his hands during a film shoot, what James did when he looked at me through framed fingers on the dock that day before he started drawing.

Maybe Amanda is afraid of losing our friendship too. Maybe that's what her anger was about that day—that I'd be so quick to say I'd leave her. Of course, I was just saying I wanted to get out of town, not that I wanted to leave her behind. But she might have taken it that way, I realize when I reframe the memory.

The other thing that occurs to me is this: she trusted me more. Whatever she has with Ethan, he's a guy she likes. Me? I'm her best friend. I'm the one she should be able to count on.

And then, out on the water, I start, for the one-thousandth time, to write the letter.

Dear Amanda,
What I did was selfish and awful, and I wish
I could take it back. I know it will take a

long time for you to trust me again, but our friendship means too much to me to let go.

The thing is, you are more than my friend. I can picture us as roommates in our dream city in our twenties, being bridesmaids in each other's weddings, renting vacation houses together with our families.

You _are_ my family. And families fracture and fight, but if there's enough love, they always come back together. Maybe not in the same way, but still strong, still connected.

I will do anything I can to show you that I am the person you thought I was. I am your Clem, your true friend forever.

Love,
Me

"Clem!" Olive is shouting for me, but I'm still in the inlet, really close to the boat.

"Olive, tell Mom I'm coming in a sec," I yell back.

My little sister studies my face and then nods, going back below deck. I reread what I wrote.

There are lots of things that I'm unsure about—where I want to go to college, whether I should keep working at Razzy's or get a more "important" job to build my résumé, whether James and I will work out off the water. But Amanda and me? We're a sure thing.

So this time, I don't tear out the page with my letter-attempt on it. I smile as I close my journal and motor back to *The Possibility*.

chapter thirty-eight

We stay at the marina another night, just to make sure things are okay with the Townsends, and the next day Dad makes two extra breakfasts. He and I take the plates over to James's boat.

Mr. Townsend meets us in the cockpit, and he and James reach over and ask us to join them.

We're about to climb aboard when George and Ruth shuffle by on their morning walk. George lets out a low whistle as he points to the back of the boat. "You finally let her go, huh, Bill?"

I freeze, thinking about the scraped-off name and wondering how Mr. Townsend will react.

Everyone else seems suspended for a moment too. Then Ruth catches up to George and says, "We've been telling you to rename that boat for months! So what'll it be?"

Her impish grin and the twinkle in George's eye make the moment lighter, more fun.

Dad hops onto the dock and walks over to look at where the lettering used to be. "You did get it pretty cleanly off of there, Bill."

"George, do you still have that gold paint you offered me last fall?" asks Mr. Townsend.

Ruth has already turned back toward their boat. "I'll get it!" she shouts.

The rest of us talk about possible names while Ruth hunts for the paint. After a few minutes of insanely lame suggestions from Dad (like, *Father & Sun* and *Fresh Start*), I go grab Mom and Olive—I know they wouldn't want to miss this renaming ceremony.

"*Winds of Change?*"

"*Rising Tide?*"

"*Lucky Guys?*"

"*Fanta-sea?*"

We're all spouting out boat names and laughing at each one. None feel right, but Ruth is back with the gold marine paint and Mr. Townsend has already started sanding down the surface where James will sketch the new name—he knows how to do these really cool looping letters.

The day wears on, and around noon, Dad goes back to our boat and makes sandwiches for everyone so we can picnic while we brainstorm. Then Olive gets silly and starts suggesting food names based on our lunch, like *Peanut Butter & Jelly* and *Pickle Juice* and *Cool Ranch*.

Mr. Townsend has been pretty quiet the whole time, but he's smiling. When he finishes up his sandwich, he looks at James and says, "What about *Clean Slate?*"

James nods as a grin starts to spread across his face. "Sounds like a good idea to me."

We all nod—if they love it, that's it. It sounds hopeful, forward looking, and kind of adventurous. I'm sure James is also glad it doesn't include a bad pun.

Ruth hands James a brush.

"Let me map it out first," he says, walking to the back of the boat and staring at the smooth surface.

A few minutes later, we all watch James sketch the first few letters, and after a half hour, Ruth and George say good-bye and stroll back to their boat. Then Mom and Dad head toward *The Possibility*. Olive and I linger a while. She's respectfully quiet as James bites his lip in concentration, making each paint stroke slowly and deliberately. I love watching him do this—it feels like he's creating a new beginning.

The sun gets lower in the sky, and although I don't want to go, this isn't a me-and-James moment.

"Olive," I say. "We should probably . . ." I lean my head toward *The Possibility*.

"Oh," she says, like she's waking up from a dream. "Okay."

I say good-bye quietly to Mr. Townsend, who's been at James's shoulder all this time, and he gives me a warm smile.

James doesn't look up, but that doesn't worry me. He's in a zone.

"Thank you," says Mr. Townsend, his hand on my shoulder.

I nod and take Olive's hand as we walk home.

chapter thirty-nine

James and I agreed that we'd meet up in two days, at the last stop we're both making on this loop. He needs some time with his dad, alone. I get that. His uncle is meeting them with a boat trailer at the final marina so they can drive back up to Illinois in time for James to start school. My grandparents from North Carolina are doing the same for us.

We'll say good-bye there. Or we'll say, "See you later," because that's all I can possibly bear to say to James. How do you say good-bye to someone who helped you put the broken pieces of your life back together? You don't.

"Clem, will you juice this lemon?" asks Mom. She's chopping up garlic on the yellow plastic cutting board.

"Sure." I grab the citrus squeezy thing from the galley drawer. "What are we making?"

"Chicken salad with fresh cucumber-yogurt dressing," says Mom. "It's Jamie Oliver's recipe."

"Whoa—you're making quite a leap from canned beans to the Naked Chef."

Jamie Oliver is this amazingly cute British guy who has a Food Network show. Amanda and I used to watch it all the time—the Food Network is kind of like meditation, I think. You can zone out and watch the rhythm of the preparations. It's nice.

"Well, our last dinner on the boat should be special," says Mom.

"James is coming over!" squeals Olive, clomping down the stairs from the cockpit.

"I know," I say, pressing the lemon tighter to get more juice. My grin is huge.

Just as the sun starts to go down, I hear the tune to that old song "Dock of the Bay" in a whistle coming from the dock.

I peek out of the cabin and see Mr. Townsend and James walking toward us. Mr. Townsend looks cheerful and bright in his yellow button-down shirt. James's hair is flaming red against the gray-washed dock and the pale greenish water. It's blowing slightly in the wind. He's wearing the blue polo that makes his eyes look like the sky, and his smile is bigger than I've ever seen it. My heart flutters.

When they get to the boat, I don't even care that our parents are right there. I pull him in for a hug as soon as he steps aboard. I bury my head in his shirt and breathe in the smell of the hand-washing detergent he uses. It's the best scent in the world.

"Hey," he says softly as he kisses the top of my head.

"I got us something," I say, and Olive hands up two frosty root beers in glass bottles. We saw them today at the dock deli, and it felt like a sign.

"My favorite," he says.

When I back away, he takes my hand, and he doesn't let it go until we get our plates for dinner.

We eat in the cockpit because it's a cool night and the breeze is perfect—light and steady, a gentle wind. The chicken salad is refreshing and tangy. Olive and I tell Mom that we're proud of her, and we even get the guys to join in on a round of applause.

"It was a group effort!" shouts Mom above the clapping. Then, she stage-whispers to me, "Does this mean no one wants the *Man, Can, Plan* dinners ever again?"

I nod. "Those are over."

When Mom brings out fresh strawberries for dessert, Mr. Townsend asks if he can make a toast, and we all raise our drinks.

"I want to thank Olive for her dogged cheer this summer," he says. My sister beams.

"And Julia, your dinner company and your sailing stories are unparalleled in my extensive experience at sea!"

Mom blushes.

"Clem," he continues. "I think you stole something from my boat, but I don't mind."

I look at him questioningly.

"James's heart," he says. I start to redden, but then James reaches over and squeezes my hand.

"And Captain Rob," he says, raising his glass higher as he turns to my dad. I stealthily take out my phone and snap a photo of the two of them. "Father to father . . ." Mr. Townsend pauses for a minute and I can see that he's getting emotional. "Well, I'm grateful," he says, leaving it at that.

We all clink our drinks together and I think of that phrase, "All is right with the world."

But in a minute, my world is going to reel.

I'm acutely aware that with each passing second, each shared glance, each touch of James's hand on mine—we get closer to saying good-bye, or so long, or however you want to put it. My heart feels so whole right now, but I know it's going to break a little before the night is over.

I've got the list I wrote tucked in my back pocket, the list of things I love about James. I added a few:

> You take care of your father.
>   You are as brave as anyone I've ever known.
>   Your hands make me feel electric.

That last thing made me nervous to write, *ack*, but I want to put it in there anyway, because it's true.

Our parents are deep in boat stories now, and I know Mom and Dad will miss Mr. Townsend back at home. None of their other close friends sail.

"Want to take a walk?" James whispers low in my ear so no one else hears.

"Yeah," I say.

I stand up and so does he. Then Olive does too.

"Livy, how about helping me clear the dishes?" asks Mom.

"Is Clem helping?" asks Olive, looking over at me as I head for the dock.

"Nope," says Mom. "You are."

I look back at Mom and give her a big smile.

She winks at me and scoots Olive into the cabin with a serving dish.

I take James's hand.

When we step off the boat, I take a deep breath. I already feel like I want to cry, but James doesn't let me.

"So, I was thinking about when you ran into me and I had all those bananas," he says.

"You mean when *you* ran into me?" I ask with a smile.

We walk up toward the end of the dock, where there's an open slip.

"Semantics," says James. "Anyway, I was thinking about all these things—like that you were wearing a white tank top and had a bathing suit on underneath, which is how I knew you were a real boat girl, and that your upper lip is shaped like the top half of a heart and your bottom lip is shaped like a canoe, kind of—"

He pauses then, and traces my mouth. As soon as his fingers get close, I shiver with the best kind of chill. And then we're both leaning in, letting our lips part as we fall into each other. His hands move to my sides, underneath my soft cotton tank, and he strokes my bare skin as I pull him closer. Shifting his hands up along my back, he playfully pulls on my bikini top strings. I take in a sharp breath, wishing we were below deck in his room.

When we finally stop to breathe, I smile. "You noticed all that in that dock deli?"

"I noticed it all in lightning time," says James. "My mind works really fast."

"Yeah, I know that about you," I say, laughing.

We sit down on the bench and James keeps talking. Surprise.

"And later when I was drawing you and I noticed—" he starts.

"That I was sad," I finish.

"Huh?" asks James.

"You noticed that I was sad."

"Oh, that, yeah, well, I noticed that in the first instant, too—at the store," he says. "It was your eyes."

"What do you mean?" I ask, looking up at him.

He shrugs. "They were just far away," he says. "The first few times I met you, you weren't here. You were somewhere else."

I nod, thinking about how much time I spent during the early part of this boat trip going over every detail of what had happened with Ethan and Amanda. I thought about it so much that I didn't even see the summer happening around me.

"I'm sorry," I say, regretful of the time I wasted.

"It's okay," says James. "You were figuring things out."

I bite my lip and look out at the water.

"What is it?" James asks.

"I just feel like everything I went through, all the stupid drama . . . you've just been through so much more and you don't act half as bratty," I say.

"Not even a *quarter* as bratty!" says James. Then he laughs. "I'm kidding. But you can't compare stuff like that."

"Yeah, but when I met you I thought you'd never seen a sad day in your life."

"You did?"

"Yes!" I say. "I mean, you are always upbeat and whistling and just generally humming along with the most positive attitude."

"And you were, like, Brood-arella," he says, knocking my shoulder with his.

"Hey!" I protest.

"You were," he says. "Just ask Crazy Olive."

"Believe me," I say, "she made it clear that she wasn't into my mood swings this summer."

"Yeah, she's not a hold-back type."

"No." I shake my head and smile.

"Well, that didn't deter me," says James. "I liked you right away."

"Why?" I ask.

"I don't know," he says. "I just felt a connection to you. I knew you were a cool person."

"Who's done some crappy things," I say.

"Yeah, well," he says. "Who hasn't?"

I sigh.

"You can't beat yourself up anymore," he says. "And you can't compare your thing to my thing or to anyone else's thing on the how-bad-should-I-feel? scale."

"This isn't what I want to be talking about," I say.

"Good," he says. "Me neither."

Then I lean in and kiss him again.

"I just want to say one more thing," he says, interrupting my favorite part of the whole night.

"What?" I ask, tapping my leg impatiently.

"You are great—seriously. Anyone would be crazy not to want to be best friends with you."

I look up at him. "I wish I saw myself the way you see me."

"It's not the way I see you," he says. "It's the way you *are*."

That's when I remember the paper in my pocket.

"Speaking of that," I say, "I have something for you."

I hand him the folded-up note.

"Now or later?" he asks.

"Now." I watch him read the list I wrote, his eyes lighting up at each line. He laughs a couple of times.

"This one's Olive's?" he asks about "You make Clem smile."

"Yup," I say. "But it's true."

I take out my phone—which I'm still in the habit of having in my pocket—and snap one more summer shot.

chapter forty

The sixteen-hour car ride with my grandparents was pretty intense. Olive and I got the way backseat of their huge SUV, so at least I could zone out and listen to music most of the ride. Olive would poke my arm if someone asked me a question, but mostly people left me alone. I wonder if Mom or Grandma ever had to say good-bye to a guy who made their summer.

I feel a buzz and reach into my back pocket to grab my cell phone.

James: u home? can't wait to see you again

Okay, so maybe we didn't really say good-bye. We said, "See you." And since he lives about forty miles away, we plan to get together next weekend. I guess we're seeing how it goes.

I smile at the screen and text back, home. miss you already

Then I sigh and look around. My room is just as I left it. Books in order on the bookshelf, flower comforter spread neatly on the bed, wicker laundry basket still with that stray gray sweatshirt sitting on top of it, waiting to be washed.

I unpack and lie on my bed for a while, staring up at the ceiling and waiting to get my land legs back—it still seems like I'm rocking back and forth.

The house is really quiet and still with all of us in our separate rooms. I can hear Dad putting things away in the kitchen—he's clanging the pots around—but it's distant and muffled, unlike everything on the boat.

I feel a little sad not to be out on the water anymore, but mostly what I feel is different. I take out my journal and reread the letter I wrote out on the dinghy. I add just one thing to the very beginning:

I'm so sorry.

That seems like the way to start. Without defenses, without excuses.

I grab my laptop, and the first thing I do is find the folder called "Every Once in a While." I drag it right into the trash.

Then I log onto Facebook. There's a friend request from Ruth—her photo is Mrs. Ficklewhiskers. The message says, "You're a sailor girl I'm proud to know. Let's keep in touch!"

Usually I think older people friend-requesting me is weird, but this one's a connection I'm glad to have. I smile and accept.

Then I click over to the message box and open Amanda's "BITCH" note—I can't ignore it any longer. It has just two sentences:

"You really hurt me. I hope you know that."

I sit back.

"Huh," I say audibly, even though I'm alone.

The message feels much less angry than I thought it was going to. It seems almost . . . reparable. Maybe we aren't broken.

I plug my phone into the computer and download the measly six shots I got over the summer. I wish I'd taken more, I think, as they transfer to the desktop.

I click to open them all at once.

"They're perfect," says Olive.

I turn around, startled.

"You have to knock, Livy," I say, but I'm not mad. I was actually getting lonely after being all by myself in this big room for almost an hour.

She ignores me.

"They're the whole summer," she says, still staring at my screen.

I look back to the photos.

Ruth and James, talking on the dock.

Olive with binoculars, spying on James.

James sketching by the water.

Mom in the morning light on The Possibility.

Mr. Townsend, raising a glass to Dad.

James's smile as he reads my love list.

I open Facebook again. I'm not ready to respond to Amanda, but I will very soon, after I polish the draft in my journal.

I click in my status box and type, "Best Summer Ever."

acknowledgments

Big hugs of gratitude to . . .

My editor, Caroline Abbey, who is wise and enthusiastic (a great combo) and who helped me map out the back story of this book with paper and scissors spread across a café table.

My agent, Doug Stewart, who freely admits that he can lose himself in teenage love stories, which is a very winning quality.

The whole team at Bloomsbury—especially ace publicists Katy Hershberger and Kate Lied—for thoughtful support of this book (and that dreamy cover).

All the blog readers who helped me think of boat names for this book—you guys are so creative and fun. Special nods to babygirlG, Jenners, and Sirena, who gave me names I used!

Chris Tebetts, who had an amazing title suggestion that fit Clem's story perfectly.

Kristina Vrouwenvelder, for being an awesome first-draft reader who called me out on the boat-trip details I missed.

Mom, for the river-route details! And Dad, for the e-mails from years ago when they took this boat trip, which I referenced daily as I wrote.

Dave, June, and my whole family, always, plus the friends who've shown me what that last *F* in BFF really means.